Published in Nashville, Tennessee by Tommy Nelson®, a Division of Thomas Nelson, Inc. Visit us on the web at www.tommynelson.com

Tommy Nelson® books may be purchased in bulk for educational, business, fundraising, or sales promotional use. For information, please email SpecialMarkets@ThomasNelson.com.

Scripture quotations are from the *International Children's Bible®, New Century Version®:* Copyright © 1986, 1988, 1999 by Tommy Nelson®, a Division of Thomas Nelson, Inc.

Creative director: Robin Crouch
Storyline development & series continuity: Dandi Daley Mackall
Computer programming consultant: Lucinda C. Thurman

Library of Congress Cataloging-in-Publication Data

Mackall, Dandi Daley.
    Please reply! / written by Dandi Daley Mackall ; created by Terry K. Brown.
        p. cm. - (TodaysGirls.com ; 8)
    Summary: As fifteen-year-old Jamie becomes involved in the swim team and Special Olympics coaching, as part of her effort to fit in and be normal, she tries to remember to talk to God.
    ISBN 0-8499-7683-9
    ISBN 1-4003-0762-7 (2005 edition)
    [Self-acceptance—Fiction. 2. Physically handicapped—Fiction. 3. Mentally handicapped—Fiction. 4. Special Olympics—Fiction. 5. Swimming—Fiction. 6. Christian Life—Fiction.] I. Brown, Terry, 1961– II. Title. III. Series.

PZ7.M1905 P1 2001
[Fic]—dc21   00-067870
                                                                          CIP

Printed in the United States of America

05 06 07 08 09 BANTA 9 8 7 6 5 4 3 2 1

PLEASE REPLY!

CREATED BY
Terry K. Brown

WRITTEN BY
Dandi Daley Mackall

Tommy nelson™
A Division of Thomas Nelson, Inc.
www.tommynelson.com
www.ThomasNelson.com

Web Words

2 to/too

4 for

ACK! disgusted

AIMP always in my prayers

A/S/L age/sex/ location

B4 before

BBL be back later

BBS be back soon

BD big deal

BF boyfriend

BFN bye for now

BRB be right back

BTW by the way

CU see you

Cuz because

CYAL8R see you later

Dunno don't know

Enuf enough

FWIW for what it's worth

FYI for your information

G2G or **GTG** I've got to go

GF girlfriend

GR8 great

H&K hug and kiss

IC I see

IN2 into

IRL in real life

JK just kidding

JLY Jesus loves you

JMO just my opinion

K okay

Kewl cool

KOTC kiss on the cheek

L8R later

LOL laugh out loud

LTNC long time no see

LY love you

NBD no big deal

NU new/knew

NW no way

OIC oh, I see

QT cutie

RO rock on

ROFL rolling on floor laughing

RU are you

SOL sooner or later

Splain explain

SWAK sealed with a kiss

SYS see you soon

Thanx (or) **thx** thanks

TNT till next time

TTFN ta ta for now

TTYL talk to you later

U you

U NO you know

UD you'd (you would)

UR your/you're/ you are

WB welcome back

WBS write back soon

WTG way to go

Y why

(Note: Remember that capitalization may vary.)

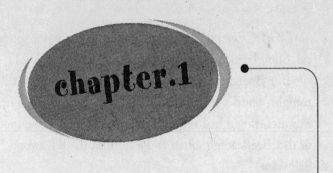

chapter.1

You can do it, Chandler! Jamie told herself as she cut between tables, tray hoisted above one shoulder the way her boss, Mr. Cross, had taught her. *One funny comment. That's all. Think! What would Bren say?*

Country Western blared from the jukebox, twang and heartbreaks bouncing off the chrome decor of the Gnosh Pit, every high school kid's favorite hangout. Jamie inhaled the stench of burned cheese and smoke that wafted from the kitchen. Morgan, the boss's daughter, had been helping in the kitchen again.

Jamie could find Morgan blindfolded, just following the aroma of burned anything. And locating Bren's table at the Gnosh wasn't much harder. Jamie just walked toward the wisecracks that never failed to bring bursts of laughter from Bren's groupies.

"Barf?" Even saying *barf,* Bren Mickler's voice sounded musical. She'd been Jamie's best friend since middle school.

But Bren had millions of friends. She couldn't help it. Like tonight. She'd strutted into the Gnosh with Chad. But after two minutes, they'd had to pull tables together to make room for half of the cheerleading squad and a third of the Edgewood High football team.

Jamie stopped behind Bren's chair. *OK, God,* she prayed, taking a deep breath. *All I'm asking for here is a great one-liner.*

Still thinking, she shifted the tray. *Nice night out? Check out those leaves? Why do they call it "fall"?* Everything she thought of to say to these popular kids sounded lame.

"Spew!"

"We have that one already, Chad!" Bren said. "Pay attention, big fella."

"Yack!" Zandrea shouted. Zandrea's straight navy skirt was shorter than her cheerleading uniform. Her long black hair hung straight to her shoulders, like Bren's.

"And how about 'lose your lunch'?" Chad asked, leaning back in his chair.

Jamie cleared her throat. "Great for business, Bren. What are you doing anyway?"

"Jamie's right, Chad," Maya scolded. "You're gross! Are you trying to put my dad out of business?" Maya, Morgan's older sister, paused and retied her silk neck scarf. The wild snake-print fuchsia perfectly complemented her creamy dark skin.

"How about 'toss your cookies'?" Maya suggested.

Bren laughed and twisted around to face Jamie. "Can you believe this? I'll have more homonyms than anybody in our sophomore English class. Won't Miss Roberts freak?"

"Synonyms, Bren," Amber corrected. "Not homonyms." It wasn't a put-down. Amber Thomas wasn't the put-down type. She'd been the one who had created the TodaysGirls.com Web site so her friends would have a safe place to chat online, free from the weirdoes who sometimes popped up in other teen chat rooms. Amber, a junior, had included Jamie, Bren, and even Maya's little sister, Morgan, and her best friend, Alex.

"Synonyms," Amber continued. "Words that mean the same thing as your given word."

"My given word was *vomit*," Bren explained to Jamie and the customers grinning from surrounding tables. "What word did you get, Jamie?"

"Normal," Jamie muttered, embarrassed at the irony. Miss Roberts had forced them to draw a word out of her lunchbox. Jamie had been staring out the window, wondering how many of the other students had to go to work after school, then race home to baby-sit and cook dinner for their family. And then she, the least normal person in the room, maybe in all Edgewood, had drawn *normal.*

As Bren laughed, her dark hair swished side-to-side, staying perfectly turned under, a living shampoo commercial. As usual, Jamie had scooped her neglected blonde hair into a ponytail.

Still balancing the tray on one hand, Jamie reached up to brush a loose strand out of her face.

"So do we get our food or what?" Zandrea asked. "I could eat an entire Brazilian rain forest. I'm a vegetarian."

"Sorry," Jamie said. She lowered the tray but lost her balance. Plates slid across the tilted tray. Jamie grabbed to make the save. A glass toppled, crashing into the ice cream dish. Chocolate ice cream flipped off the tray and into Chad's lap.

"Hey!" Chad stood up, knocking over his chair. Clumps of chocolate plopped from his baggy jeans to the floor.

Jamie plunked her tray onto the table and grabbed a handful of napkins. She started to wipe Chad's jeans, stopped, then bent down to pick up the ice cream with her bare hands. "Man, I'm sorry, Chad. What an idiot!"

Bren held out the dish so Jamie could let go of the freezing fistful of ice cream. "I thought *I* was the spaz around here," Bren said, laughing as if this were no more than nightly Gnosh entertainment.

Jamie shrugged. *Great. I try to be more like Bren and end up with her only fault.* Actually, even clumsiness worked for Bren. People thought of it as cute.

Jamie patted her hands with the paper napkins, but she couldn't get all the stickiness off. The napkins stuck between her fingers instead. *This* was definitely not cute.

Assorted hands reached across the table and grabbed the hamburgers and fries until nothing remained on the tray except smushed ice cream. "I'll get you a new bowl, Chad," Jamie said.

"Not hand-dipped this time, if you don't mind," Chad called.

When Jamie returned with a generous ice cream replacement, Maya and Amber were really getting into Bren's assignment.

"I know, I know!" Maya squealed. "Hurl!"

"Go, Maya!" Bren cried, adding "hurl" to her list.

"Sweet, Maya," Amber said. "I'm sure your dad appreciates your vocabulary. Wait . . . *regurgitate! Automatic reflex of the over-stimulated vestibular apparatus.*"

Jamie laughed along with everybody. But her mind ground through its gears trying to come up with even one word for Bren's list. "Do you have puke?" she asked softly.

"Only about an hour ago," Zandrea replied.

The tall, thin guy across from Bren cocked his head and narrowed huge green eyes at Jamie. "I know you," he said.

Jamie knew him. David Early, starting quarterback. She risked a glance at him, then looked back at the overflowing bowl of ice cream and wished she had Bren's wit. Or Bren's hair. Or Bren's anything.

"Got it!" David said. "You're on the swim team, right?"

Zandrea laughed. Zandrea swam with Bren, Amber, Maya, and the other *normal* swimmers. "Nope. Jamie helps Coach Short at our practices."

"Is Coach Short your dad?" David asked. "You kind of remind me of him."

Jamie felt her cheeks on fire as Zandrea burst into giggles. Coach Harry Short was short . . . and bald. Jamie was 5'4", 120 pounds, and she had hair! She loved Harry like a father, but looking like him was not on her wish list.

Amber spoke up for her. "Jamie does everything for the swim team. We couldn't get along without her, and neither could Coach."

"Do you know how to swim, Jamie?" Zandrea asked. "I don't think I've ever seen you suit up." When Zandrea smiled, her teeth flashed a bluish whiteness that Jamie knew could only come from a deep wallet.

Jamie swallowed hard. *I wanted them to notice me. But not like this.*

"Actually," she said, resting a worn tennis shoe on Bren's chair leg and absently wadding the napkins, "I'm thinking of joining the swim team. You know, being a regular, normal type swimmer."

The second she'd said it, her heart pounded. She hadn't been thinking any such thing.

"Jamie!" Bren exclaimed, jumping out of her chair for a quick hug. "That rocks! You're already a better swimmer than I am."

"She sure makes more of the practices than you do," Maya quipped. "Seriously, girl? We can use you."

"Sweet! Have you told Coach yet?" Amber asked.

It was happening too fast. Jamie needed time to think. She couldn't keep up. "I better get back to work before I get fired," she said, backing away, trying to look casual.

Oomph! Jamie backed into someone. She turned to see Alex Diaz, the newest member of TodaysGirls.com.

"Watch where you're going there, Jamie," Alex said. "What's up?" Alex looked like she always did—attractive grunge. If Jamie had worn those baggy jeans or that plaid flannel shirt, she'd have looked like a bag lady. But even with wild hair and no makeup, Alex's fiery beauty made guys do double takes.

"Sorry, Alex," Jamie said.

"Squirrel-tossing!"

"Making soup!"

"Returning the mail?"

Alex frowned at Bren's table. "Somebody want to clue me in?"

"Alex!" Bren cried, as if she hadn't seen her for a year. "We need words and phrases for throwing up."

Alex, not bothering to ask why, pulled over a chair from the next table, making it screech against the floor, and straddled it backward. "Blowing chunks."

"Good one!" Bren squealed.

Even Alex fits in better than I do, Jamie thought as she turned toward the kitchen. *And she doesn't even try.*

"Jamie?" Bren called after her. "Where are you going?"

"Some of us have to work," Jamie said, forcing a chuckle.

"Take your break with us, OK?" Bren asked. "I *need* you!"

"And, hey," Alex added. "Will you bring me a shake then?"

Jamie nodded. As she walked away, she heard Maya tell Alex about Jamie's trying out for the swim team. Jamie hadn't planned to say that. The words had just come out—no brain involved.

Maybe it's meant to be, she thought, heading for the kitchen.

Maybe joining the swim team will be the first step to an all-new, all-normal life for Jamie Chandler.

Jamie had just ripped off an order and passed it to Morgan when she heard her mother's voice. She pivoted in time to see Mom and Jessica, her little sister, gawking around for an empty table.

"Mom?" Jamie said, hurrying up to them. "Why are you here?"

Mom shouted above the Gnosh noise, "Do you greet all your customers like this?"

"Sorry." Jamie reached down and hugged Jess. She liked the way her sister's coal black hair always smelled like peaches. Jamie loved both of her sisters—Jordan, age 12, and Jessica, 9. But Jessica felt like a physical part of her, a second heart.

"So, are you here for ice cream because you aced a test?" Jamie asked, helping Jess wriggle out of her backpack.

"Hardly," Mom said. "See if you can take your break now, will you, Jamie? I want you in on this."

There goes my normal break, Jamie thought.

Mr. Cross gave her fifteen minutes, and Jamie grabbed a back booth, sliding in next to Jess. Mom looked worn out. Jamie thought her mother was pretty, for a mom. But dark circles weighed down her usually bright blue eyes. Jamie knew Janet Chandler's life wasn't any more normal than her daughter's. She had to raise three kids on her own, working full time as a paralegal and studying law on the side.

"Your sister," Mom began, the familiar hint of controlled anger edging every word, "is in trouble at school."

Jamie laughed. "*This* sister?" Jordan was the one who got in trouble. Not Jessica. "What for? Giving away her jellybeans? Saving a place in line?"

"It's not funny," Mom said, eyes fixed on Jessica, who hadn't said a word.

Morgan set a pitcher of Coke on the table. "Dad said you guys looked thirsty." She winked at Jessica and got a huge grin back.

"That's sweet of you—and your father, Morgan," Mrs. Chandler said. "Tell him thanks for us."

Jamie poured while her mom listed Jessica's crimes. "Your sister hasn't been completing her assignments. Her teacher says she's stopped paying attention in class. She doesn't listen."

Jamie turned in the booth to face her sister. "Jessica, that doesn't sound like you."

Jess shrugged and sipped her Coke.

Mom leaned across the table, her hands gripping the chrome edge. "And I got a call from the principal tonight. Do you want to tell your sister about it, Jess?"

Still silent, Jessica stirred her Coke with a straw.

"Fine." Mom's voice grew sharper. "Jessica got hauled into the office for hiding out during recess. She didn't come in when the whistle blew. They had to go out and get her. She was sitting behind that spirea bush, reading as if she hadn't a care in the world!"

Jamie couldn't help laughing. "No way! Jessica? Our Jess?"

"It's not funny, Jamie!" Mom insisted. "The principal didn't think it was funny."

Jamie swallowed the giggles that wanted to bubble out. "Jess," she said, gaining control, "what's up with you, kid?"

Jessica shrugged again.

Mom slumped back in her seat. "See? I can't get her to talk to me, Jamie! That's why I brought her to you." She glanced at her watch. "Rats! I have to go back to the office. It's Ms. Reynolds again, the new partner. Can I leave Jessica? Maybe she'll talk to you when you get off."

"Sure," Jamie said. "No sweat, Mom. I'll talk to her. You know Jess. She'll be fine." Jess smiled at her sister.

Mom thanked Jamie and kissed Jessica's head before she rushed out the door. Jamie watched her mom through the window as she crossed the parking lot to their aging car. They waved good-bye, then Jamie put in a special order of chili-cheese fries, Jessica's favorite.

Jamie wasn't too worried. Of all the Chandlers, Jessica had the best shot at having a normal life. Their dad had left them before Jess was even born, so she had that one Chandler strike against her. But Jess was gorgeous and popular. Jamie felt sure her little sister had what it took to be another Bren.

When Jamie returned with Jessica's fries, Bren was sitting across from Jess, who was giggling so hard her eyes watered. Jamie suspected that Bren was Jess's favorite human.

Bren stretched across the table. "There she is, Jess," she said. "You want to tell her, or should I?"

"You!" Jess cried, grinning back at Bren.

"OK. Jamie, Jess and I are volunteering you to help with Special Olympics swimming."

"Bren—" Jamie started.

"Sorry. You've been volunteered," Bren said. "You'll love it! Dad's sponsoring the team. I picked out these awesome purple team shirts with dragons on the front. And the kids are so great!"

Jamie felt her stomach twitch. "I can't, Bren."

"Jamie!" Jess pleaded. "Please? My friend from church is on the team! You know Eddy."

"Come on, Jamie!" Bren said. "It'll be a blast!" She tapped her pink nails on the table impatiently.

"I'm not like you, Bren," Jamie protested. "I wouldn't know what to say to them. I can hardly talk to normal kids."

Jamie couldn't help feeling sorry for handicapped kids. *I'd like to help, but I'd make things worse. I'd probably cry.*

"You'll do great!" Bren insisted. "We'll teach them starts, strokes, turns, etcetera, etcetera."

Jessica sat up on her knees and put her hand on Bren's forehead. "I'm sorry, Bren. Does it hurt bad?"

Jamie and Bren exchanged puzzled glances.

"Does what hurt?" Bren asked.

"Your head," Jess answered.

"My head's fine."

"Then why do you need Excedrin?" Jessica asked.

Bren looked confused then burst into laughter. "*Etcetera*, Jess! Not Excedrin." She ruffled Jess's hair. "I wish I could take you home with me," she said, sliding out of the booth.

"As for you, Jamie Chandler." Bren tugged at her capris and

pulled down her jewel-studded denim jacket. "Special Olympics practice is at the YMCA, Saturday mornings."

Bren headed for her table of waiting fans. Then she called over her shoulder. "And if you can come up with one more throw-up expression, I'll have fifty!"

Jamie turned to Jess. "You wait right here. Don't go home without me."

Jamie kept busy until the end of her shift. In between orders, she racked her brain for one measly vomit synonym.

Finally, Maya came back to the kitchen. "I'll help finish up. Mom kidnapped Dad and drove home early." Maya grabbed a big box of toilet paper and headed to the rest rooms to restock for Jamie.

Then it came to Jamie. "Drive the porcelain bus!" she cried. She ran back to Bren's table to give them #50 on the vomit list, but it was too late. They'd all gone home.

Jamie trudged back to the booth to tell Jessica to get ready to leave. But Jess wasn't in her seat.

Jamie glanced around the empty Gnosh. "Jess?" she yelled. She checked the bathroom. "Jessica! You in here?"

"Not in here," Maya answered from a stall.

"What's going on?" Morgan shrieked, rushing through the door with a broom still in hand.

"Have you seen Jess? She was supposed to wait for me. I told her to stay put."

"She wouldn't walk home alone," Maya offered. "Not this

late." Jamie dashed back into the dining room, her friends close behind her.

Jamie couldn't speak. What if Jess had left a long time ago? Jamie hadn't bothered to check on her. *What if somebody stopped and picked her up? Or kidnapped her?*

Maya hollered, "Jessica!"

The name echoed in the empty Gnosh like a hollow, lonely chant.

Jamie felt as if somebody had poured cold water inside her bones, where it froze solid. "Jess," she whispered, "where are you?"

chapter.2

Be cool, Jamie," Maya said. "I'll call your house. Don't freak. Jessica's probably home already."

Jamie willed her legs to move. She and Morgan looked in booths, under tables, and out back, yelling Jessica's name nonstop.

Please, God, Jamie prayed, *look out for Jess wherever she is. Make her be home safe already.*

When Maya came out from the kitchen, Jamie could tell by her face that Jessica wasn't home.

"Nobody answered at your house," Maya said.

"Where could she be? I told her *not* to go home without me. I told her to stay put." Jamie forced back the tears. "What if somebody—"

"Don't even go there," Maya said.

"Let's split up and search outside," Morgan suggested.

Please Reply!

They filed out of the Gnosh, Maya locking the door behind them.

"Jessica! Where are you?" Jamie screamed.

Morgan and Maya circled the Gnosh in opposite directions, calling for Jess, while Jamie scoured the parking lot, asking the few stragglers if they'd seen a little girl with black hair and a brown jacket.

An icy autumn wind blew in gusts that felt like cold slaps as Jamie peered under parked cars and behind trees.

"No luck?" Maya called, jogging back.

"Didn't see her," Morgan said, dodging the bike rack. She kicked at fallen leaves as if Jessica might be hiding under them.

Jamie trotted over to them. "This isn't like Jess. She had to know I'd go crazy looking for her."

"Maybe she got lost," Morgan suggested.

"Not Jess," Jamie said. "She's got the best sense of direction in our family."

"Come on!" Maya said, running to the parking lot. "We'll take Mr. Beep and drive around. Maybe Jessica's on her way home now. Maybe she just hasn't gotten there yet."

"Where's Jordan?" Morgan asked, trying to keep up.

Jamie shook her head. "I have no idea. I just know Mom's at the law office. Think I should call her?"

Maya unlocked her Volkswagen bug, and they climbed over the magazines strewn across the seat. "Let's drive to your house and see if we find Jessica. If we don't, you can call your mom from there."

Maya drove slowly while Morgan and Jamie hung their heads out the window and hollered for Jessica.

At the first stoplight, somebody pulled up behind them and honked.

Jamie squinted at the car. "It's Harry!" she yelled, waving her arms out the window. "Harry!"

"Coach!" Morgan cried.

Coach Short got out of his car and ran up to Jamie's window. "Are you OK?" he asked. He frowned in through the windshield. "Maya, you're driving two miles an hour."

"Jess is gone, Harry!" Jamie said, and the tears came. "Mom left her with me at the Gnosh. I told her to stay put. When I finished my shift, she wasn't there. Do you think—"

"Slow down, Jamie," he said softly, putting his hand on her shoulder. "I'm sure Jessica's fine. She's got a level head. There's probably a good explanation."

Behind them, horns honked. Coach waved them around, and three cars pulled through the green light.

"And you have a nice night, too," Maya muttered at the angry drivers.

"Maya," Coach said, leaning in through the window. "Drive Jamie home. I'll follow you. We'll find Jessica. Don't worry."

Coach jogged to his car. Then he followed Maya the block and a half to Jamie's.

Maya pulled into the driveway, and Jamie jumped out before

Mr. Beep had stopped rolling. She raced up the porch steps and threw open the front door. "Jess!" she hollered. "Jessica!"

Jordan got up from the couch and met Jamie in the entryway. "Boy, are you going to be in trouble when Mom gets home. I wouldn't—"

Jamie grabbed her sister's shoulders. "Jordan, have you seen Jess?"

Jordan shook her off. "Duh, yeah."

"When? Where?"

Behind her, in the doorway, Jamie heard Harry scrambling in with Morgan and Maya.

"Where?" Jordan repeated. "Here. Where you sent her, even though Mom wouldn't have let Jessica walk home alone. Jess said you told her to go home."

Jamie felt hope filling her like helium. "She's here?" Jamie tore down the hall and threw open the door to Jess and Jordan's room.

There was Jessica, already in her pink nightgown, sitting up in bed reading. Jamie ran and scooped her little sister into her arms.

"Don't *ever* do that again, Jess," she said, her body shaking with relief. "Why? Why did you come home without me?"

"You told me to, Jamie," Jess said. "It was scary, too. But I said that Twenty-third Psalm a hundred times, about walking in dark valleys and not being afraid. And I picked up a stick and pretended it was my rod and staff."

"I never said to—"

Maya knocked at the door and stuck her head in. "Everything ok? Hey, Jess. You gave us a scare! Jamie, if you're cool, Morgan and I better get back to the Gnosh and finish cleaning up."

Jamie walked Maya back to the living room, where Coach and Morgan were still waiting. "I'm sorry, you guys," Jamie said. "Jessica misunderstood me, I guess. Thanks for everything. Sorry I got crazy."

"No kidding," Jordan muttered.

Jamie wheeled on Jordan, remembering the call to the house. "Why didn't you answer the phone, Jordan? Maya called to see if Jess was here."

Jordan sneered but didn't answer.

"Listen, we'll get out of here now," Coach said, herding Morgan and Maya through the door. "You girls should go to bed early."

"Talk to you online tonight, Jamie," Morgan called back.

Once they were gone, Jamie honed in on Jordan. "You're not getting out of this so easily. Why didn't you answer the phone?"

Jordan bared her teeth, which had only that morning been wired with new braces. "*That's* why!" she said, pointing to the wire brackets fencing in each tooth. "I told Mom I didn't want braces. And until they're off, I'm not answering phones. I'm never smiling again. No way am I saying one word at school! Just listen to the way I talk! I sound like a spit machine! Besides, Jessica could have answered the phone."

Jordan stormed back to her room.

Now that the terror was over, Jamie remembered to tell God

thanks. She'd been trying to pray more, to have the on-the-spot prayer connection with God that she knew Amber had. She was getting the hang of it, but she had a long way to go.

A glance at her watch told her she had an hour to kill before the scheduled chat.

Her only homework was the same assignment Bren had been working on. During lunch hour, Jamie had come up with half a dozen words for *normal*. Unlike Bren Mickler, *she* didn't have the whole football team and cheerleading squad to help.

Maybe I can at least surf the Net and come up with more.

Jamie went to her room and turned on her computer, setting out her pajamas while the old dragon warmed up. Hers was the oldest computer in the TodaysGirls group, with the possible exception of Alex's. So everything took twice as long.

After logging on, Jamie clicked *GoTo.com*, her favorite search engine, and typed in her word for English class: *normal*. While she waited for the computer, she changed into her PJs and threw her laundry into the hamper.

When she got back to the screen, Jamie found 240 matches for *normal*.

Scrolling through the list headers, she moved down through U.S. cities and European towns named "Normal." *Too bad I wasn't born there*, she thought. *On the other hand, they'd have kicked me out by now.*

She found a "normal" newsletter that she felt sure wouldn't add her to their lists, a counseling agency called "Normal," and even a Normal University. *Won't bother applying there.*

Finally, she landed on a "Normality Web Site Study." She clicked on a picture of a normal brain and watched as the squiggly cerebral image took shape, wondering how *her* brain would look and if they had an "Abnormality Web Site."

The image was taking too long to fill in, so she clicked the Life icon. Small photos popped up on the screen, pictures of normal families: Mom, Dad, brother, sister, all smiling around the dinner table; another two-parent family driving to the beach, maybe on a family vacation. Jamie had never had a vacation, unless you counted visits to Grandma's.

She sank deeper into depression as each normal image formed, until she couldn't stand it any longer. She exited the site by typing "todaysgirls.com" in her address block and hitting *Enter*.

The familiar logo at the top of the screen made her feel she'd come home. Amber had been so right to set up the Web site. Jamie couldn't remember what they'd done before they had this safe, online home to hash over everybody's day.

She felt a pang of guilt when she saw the hot button for her part of the site: Artist's Corner. It had been two weeks since she'd added anything new. The art posted wasn't half bad—a self-portrait and five caricatures of her friends: Amber, Alex, Maya, Morgan, and Bren. Bren's had given her the most trouble since her perfect features didn't offer any natural place to exaggerate for humor.

Amber had a new Thought for the Day. Jamie leaned back in her folding chair and read:

Please Reply!

Psalm 139:13-14 says, You made my whole being. You formed me in my mother's body. I praise you because you made me in an amazing and wonderful way. What you have done is wonderful. I know this very well.

Isn't it great to know we're made-to-order by God! Awesome! When's the last time you told God, "Good job!" and gave Him credit for how cool you are?

"Easy for you to say, Amber," Jamie muttered to the screen as she clicked out of Amber's section and over to Maya's. *Maybe I should add "Amber Thomas" to my normal list,* Jamie thought.

Maya's funky, colorful Web page came together on the screen, a big banner waving across the top: What's Hot—What's Not.

WHAT'S HOT?

Minis are still in for skirts
More prints, plaids
Anything suede in ANY color
Denim jackets
Hair? Long, loose, flowing hair, mega volume! (Streaks of color, if you can pull it off)
**Rainbow eyes--tinting your disposable contacts for weird eye colors--It may be hot, but it's stupid! DO NOT DO THIS ONE! MEGA DANGEROUS!

Jamie stopped reading. She didn't wear anything in the What's Hot list. *No way I'm reading Maya's What's Not list! I'll bet I'm wearing everything on it.*

She opted against checking out Bren's Smashin' Fashion page. *Enough is enough. Besides, time to chat!*

Jamie logged on with her private chat name, rembrandt, and typed in her password. Alex (TX2step), Maya (nycbutterfly), and Morgan (jellybean) were already burning up the screen:

jellybean: said i was sorry!!

nycbutterfly: ACK! like that gives me back my granola bars.

TX2step: BD! so morgan 8 ur dum granola. get over it.

nycbutterfly: wait til I find ur M & M's, li'l sis!

Jamie could see Amber as she arrived in the chat room, too.

faithful1 is entering the room.

faithful1: ooooh . . . enuf! I M here 4 fun!

rembrandt: me 2! i could use sum fun.

nycbutterfly: hey, rembrandt! All kewl at Chandler lost & found?

jellybean: jess k?

rembrandt: yup. thanx 4 helping.

TX2step: hey, rembrandt! heard ur bucking 2B a regular in the Coach Short swimming army. r u?

Please Reply!

jellybean: RO! so kewl, rembrandt!!!! team pics r coming up. u can sit by me!!

rembrandt: i'll C. i'd like 2b a normal team member, u no?

nycbutterfly: what will Coach do w/o u as helper???? he won't B able 2 find our meets w/o u!

faithful1: ROFL! 2 true!

Jamie felt relieved when Bren showed up, late as usual, to change the subject. With the Jessica scare and all, Jamie still hadn't talked to Harry about swimming with the team.

chicChick: sorry i'm L8!

TX2step: like we're shocked, chic

chicChick: N-E-Ways--i was shopping--

nycbutterfly: Shock #2

chicChick: ACK! shopping for Special Olympics shirts! rembrandt, u r going 2 luv working w/ these kids!

Jamie wasn't so sure. She knew it was wrong, but being around the handicapped made her feel sad. And squirmy. And guilty for feeling squirmy.

From the living room, shouts and booms exploded. Jamie left the computer and ran down the hall. Music blared full blast, and TV voices shouted at each other.

Mom stood in the doorway, yelling, hands cupped around her mouth.

Jordan screamed something at Jessica, who sat cross-legged on the floor, inches from the TV.

"What's going on?" Jamie yelled.

Mom slammed the door and ducked her head, as if the horrendous noise came from dive-bombers overhead. "I asked Jordan to turn down the TV!" Mom shouted.

Jordan yelled back, "I told Jess to turn *off* the TV! Then she turned *on* the CD!"

By the time Jamie got back to her computer, chat was over, and her Internet server had disconnected her.

Figures, Jamie thought, plopping onto her bed. She opened her English notebook to her synonym assignment. At the very bottom of her list under "normal," she wrote: **Not me!**

chapter.3

Friday morning Jamie pulled on her straight-legged Levi's and a brown turtleneck sweater she'd gotten for Christmas in eighth grade. *Definitely straight out of Maya's What's Not Hot list,* she thought, checking herself out in the mirror. She brushed her hair to the side, trying to get it to part like Bren's, but her hair had other ideas.

When she found Jessica and Jordan already at the breakfast table, Jamie figured she must be running late. "Morning," she mumbled.

"Morning, Jamie," Jessica said, her mouth full of her favorite cereal, Chocolate Bunny Krisps. "Will you braid my hair for school?"

Jamie sighed. She really didn't have time.

"OK," she said, taking Jessica's angel hair and weaving it into a long braid full of wispy escapee hairs.

"And good morning to you, charming Chandler sister," Jamie said to Jordan, who still hadn't uttered a sound.

Jordan offered a tight-lipped nod, keeping her vow of silence and smile-less-ness.

"Jamie, tell your sister her braces are cute," Mom said, whisking into the kitchen, pouring a glass of orange juice, and whooshing out again.

"Cute braces, Jordan," Jamie said, pouring her cereal. The little brown pellets smelled chocolatey, but the stuff tasted like cardboard.

"More orange juice, Jess?" Jamie asked.

"Jamie," Jess said, "will you go to the mall with me this weekend? I need gym socks . . . from a sports store."

"OK, but do you want orange juice?" Jamie held the carton, ready to pour.

"I want those kind with the little balls on the heels," Jessica said.

"OK already!" Jamie said. "Orange juice?"

Jessica stared dreamy-eyed into the brownish milk at the bottom of her bowl. "Hmm? No, silly! I don't want orange. You have to wear white in gym class or Ms. Hovatter makes you run laps."

Honk! Honk! Jamie heard Coach's horn out front.

"Jamie, Harry's here!" Mom called from the living room.

"I'm coming!" Jamie choked down three more spoonfuls of the cardboard cereal, threw her dishes in the sink, and grabbed her pack.

"Jess, you be good today!" she called back. "Jordan, you too."

The girls would have another half-hour before Mom drove them to school. Harry always swung by to pick up Jamie, and sometimes the swimmers, just to make sure they didn't miss before-school practice.

This morning Jamie hoped she'd have Harry to herself. She needed to talk to him. She knew she couldn't assume he'd put her on the swim team just because she wanted him to.

Besides, special treatment wasn't what Jamie wanted, not at all. To tell the truth, she couldn't say what she did want. She liked helping Harry during practices—keeping records and organizing everything for the team. She was just tired of being the odd girl out.

A wet, gray chill greeted her as she dashed to Harry's van. Hiding her disappointment at finding Amber, Alex, and Bren already crammed inside, Jamie hollered good morning and climbed in back with Bren.

"I love it!" Bren shouted. "Jamie Chandler's late! And we picked you up last, too."

"At least we didn't have to go in and drag *her* out," Alex said.

Amber turned around from the front. "Ready to make some waves, Jamie?"

Harry pulled away from the curb, giving Jamie a quick glance in his rearview mirror. "So what's this about my losing a helper but gaining a swimmer?"

"I should have called you, Harry," Jamie said. "Listen, I don't expect you to just stick me on the team."

"Why not?" Bren asked. "You swim like a fish!"

"Maybe," Alex interrupted. "But I had to swim with you guys for weeks before I got put on the team. And Coach had all my win records from Texas."

"Two weeks, Alex," Harry said. He glanced in the rearview again. "You really want to do this, Jamie?"

"Yeah," Jamie said. "I mean, well, I just want to be a normal part of the swim team for once. When somebody asks me, 'Aren't you on the swim team?' I want to tell them yes."

"Interesting reason to want to be one of my swimmers," Coach said.

Jamie wished they were by themselves. She and Harry could talk about anything. She could make him understand.

"Can't Jamie practice with us for a while, Coach?" Amber suggested.

"Like two weeks, for example?" Alex added.

"And Jamie gets to be in the team picture, too!" Bren exclaimed. "Right, Coach?"

Coach Short sighed. "I suppose. No special favors though, Jamie. You work like everybody else on the team—except Bren. Work *harder* than Bren."

"Ouch," Bren said.

It's actually happening, Jamie thought as they wheeled into the Edgewood High faculty parkinglot. *Jamie Chandler is not just a helper anymore.*

Jamie always felt as if they were sneaking into the school on practice mornings. Harry unlocked the door, and the girls shuffled down the empty hall to the pool.

Inside the pool area, water-light danced off walls and ceiling, and words bounced in echoes as the girls plodded to the locker room. Instead of straightening Harry's office and getting out time sheets, Jamie suited up, just like the others.

Zandrea and the rest of the team straggled in, most looking half-asleep.

Morgan and Maya burst into the locker room just as Jamie tugged on her swim cap.

"Minor Mr. Beep rebellion," Maya explained, yanking her locker open. "I *hate* being late."

"You get used to it," Bren said. She still didn't have her suit on.

"You *have* to get used to being late if you're Bren's best friend," Jamie added, snapping at Bren with a towel, but missing.

Bren elbowed her. "Didn't any of you Type A's ever hear Shakespeare's famous quote: 'To be late, or not to be late—that is the question. And ye answer be: Better late than ever'?"

"It's 'Better late than *never*,'" Amber corrected, grinning. "And it wasn't Shakespeare."

"Jamie!" Morgan exclaimed, shedding her tennis shoes. "I forgot you'd be swimming with us. Cool!"

"Thanks, Morgan," Jamie said, following Amber, always first suited up. "See you out there, guys. I better check on Harry."

Harry, a frown darkening his fair complexion, was flipping through sheets on his clipboard. In his Nike sweats, Harrison Short looked like a slightly overgrown kid—reddish hair, what was left of it; freckles; and crinkles instead of wrinkles.

Bren, who stood only an inch shorter than Harry, liked to call him "Napoleon" behind his back. True, Harry tended to bark orders and run a tight ship. But for Jamie, he'd been the closest thing she'd had to a father since her parents' divorce.

"Harry!" Jamie shouted, ambling over to him. "If you're looking for time sheets, they're in your top—"

"Warmups!" Harry shouted. "And it's *Coach* to my swimmers. Give me fifteen hundred yards, everybody."

Jamie stopped in her tracks, Harry's words landing like specks of ice on her neck. It made sense, of course. Nobody on the team was allowed to call Coach Harrison Short by his nickname. But Jamie had called him Harry for as long as she could remember.

"Go! Go! Go!" Harry clapped his hands.

Half a dozen splashes echoed as swimmers dived into the pool. Jamie hustled to an open lane and stuck her toe in to test the temperature. One whiff told her somebody had put in too much chlorine.

"Har—!" Jamie started to tell Harry, then remembered that wasn't her job.

"Swim or get out of the way," Zandrea said, stepping around Jamie and diving in.

Jamie dived in after her, shivering as she came up for air. Wide awake now, she fell into an American crawl, slicing the water at an even pace.

Please, God, she prayed, making an awkward turn and transitioning into a breaststroke, *let me swim great. Help me amaze Harry and Zandrea and the whole team.*

It occurred to Jamie that she hadn't prayed since they'd found Jessica. It was just so hard to remember to talk to God.

How does Amber do it?

Jamie didn't finish warmups with the first wave of girls, but she wasn't dead last either.

Morgan angled over to her and whispered, "You did great, Jamie! See?" Morgan had finished right behind Jamie, but only because she'd been the last one in.

After the 1,500-yard warmup, Coach tried to organize the girls, running butterfly from lane one; breaststroke, lane two; backstroke, lane three; freestyle, lanes four through six. But without Jamie to help manage starts, everything took longer.

"Can't believe how tired I am!" Jamie told Bren as they headed for the lockers to change for class.

"You swam way too hard," Bren said. "Coach was a riot, wasn't he? He was so scattered, he almost made *me* look organized."

"Anybody up for the mall after school?" Zandrea asked.

"Did somebody say *mall?*" Bren asked. "I'm in!"

"How 'bout it, Jamie?" Zandrea asked over the roar of the hair dryer.

Zandrea's asking me to go to the mall with her?

Jamie tried to act cool. "I don't know," she answered, trying not to show how much she wanted to go with them. "I've got to work tonight."

"We can get you to the Gnosh on time," Bren countered.

"I'd have to go home and change before work," Jamie said.

"No problem," Zandrea said. "I've got Daddy's car. I'll take you home to change. Then Bren and I can drive you to the Gnosh and get something to eat."

Bren turned to Jamie. "Want to?"

"Sure," she said, glad she'd just deposited her Gnosh paycheck.

Zandrea leaned so close to the mirror to put on her lipstick, a circle of fog formed. "You know what I always say: 'It's not whether you win or lose. It's how you look.'" She smacked her lips, then swung around to face them. "We're on!"

"Yea!" Bren cheered. "Ooh, and there's a new cosmetic clinician at Martinique's. She's a reinvention queen!"

Jamie walked the halls of Edgewood High that morning feeling more a part of the student body than ever before.

At lunch she shoved through the lunchroom crowd, taking only salad and juice. Voices clashed as kids yelled over one another's voices. Plates clunked onto trays as Jamie sidled up to join Amber and Maya.

A second later Zandrea and Bren ran in.

"Look what we've got!" Bren exclaimed, sliding next to Jamie and spreading open a big silver book with purple lettering. "The yearbook's out!"

"Cool!" Maya said. "I ordered one. Where are they?"

"We can't officially pick them up yet," Zandrea explained, thumbing through the hefty album. "Last year's seniors can get theirs this afternoon."

"Which stinks since they're not around to have each other

sign," Amber said. "I wish we did it like my cousin's school. Their yearbooks come out in the spring."

"I only got mine because I helped on yearbook staff last year," Zandrea said. "The rest of you get them next week."

Jamie had wanted to order one, but they were too expensive.

"No!" Bren squealed, pointing to a shot of the cheerleading squad. "Look at me with my mouth wide open!"

Alex had come up and was squinting over Zandrea's shoulder. "Bren's mouth wide open?" she said dryly. "Go figure."

Bren was already on to other pages. "I can't believe I wore that dress!" she cried, slapping her hand over a picture of the homecoming dance.

"There I am!" Maya shouted. "Mmm-mmm, am I hot or what?"

"Amber," Zandrea said, holding up the page with the swim team picture, "great shot of you."

"You, too," Amber said. At the corner of the page was a small closeup of Amber and Zandrea with wet towels on their heads and their eyes crossed.

Jamie studied every page in the swim section. She remembered taking most of the action photos. It had been her idea to take one of the team shots around the boards.

A small crowd gathered at their table, with students playfully shoving each other aside for better looks at the yearbook.

"Who is that stud with the football?" Chad asked, pointing to his own team photo.

"You mean *this* stud?" Tyler asked, turning to his Quiz Bowl picture.

As she observed the others laughing and pointing out pictures, Jamie tried to join in, hoping none of them would notice what burned in her chest and made her bite her bottom lip to keep from crying: *Jamie Chandler was not in one single photograph.*

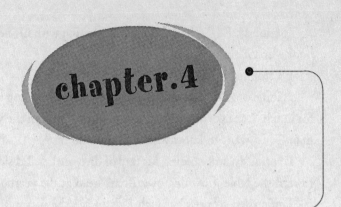

chapter.4

Jamie found herself squeezed to the outside of the crowd huddled around Zandrea's yearbook. She drank her juice and threw everything else in the trash.

When she got back to the table, Chad and Tyler had taken control of page-turning.

"Hey, Ed!" Chad yelled, slapping his hand down so Tyler couldn't turn the page. "Come over here, Ed!"

Ed Spenser, in line to dump his tray, didn't stop as he passed the table. But he slowed down and frowned suspiciously at Chad.

Jamie had seen Ed around at her church, but she'd never really talked to him. He had all LD or special needs classes, so she rarely ran into him at school. Ed was as tall as Tyler, but too skinny and angular, in baggy gray pants and a black T-shirt.

"Seriously, Ed," Chad shouted, motioning with his head to the book, "come and see this."

Ed stopped but didn't come closer.

"Come on, Ed!" Chad said, laughing. "I'm not going to eat you for lunch. Just take one look at this picture. You're in the yearbook, man. I just want to know what you were doing."

Cautiously, still holding his tray of dirty dishes, Ed sidestepped toward the table, frowning over Bren's head at the yearbook.

Jamie tried to peek through kids to see the picture. It looked like three or four guys in the gym. Ed was holding a basketball.

Ed leaned in fast, glimpsed the photo, then pulled back. "Basketball," he muttered.

"What'd he say?" Tyler asked.

Chad shrugged. "What did you say, Ed?" He shouted each word as if Ed were deaf.

Ed frowned and turned away. That's when Jamie spotted his hearing aid. A wave of sorrow burned through her, and she looked away.

"Poor Special Ed," Tyler said, flipping the yearbook to prom pages.

"Stop it!" The cry was followed by the crashing of trays dropping and dishes banging. "Quit pushing!"

Jamie turned just in time to see Ed's tray bounce on the floor, his uneaten cobbler flying in the air, then splatting onto somebody's sandals.

"Yuck! Gross! It's all over me!" Emily Eaton screamed.

"I was here in line!" Ed yelled back, angry as hornets.

"You jerk!" Emily yelled, tiptoeing as if she were walking on coals.

"*You're* the jerk!" Ed shouted, forcing in front of her in line.

"Fight!" somebody hollered.

Ed isn't deaf, Jamie thought, glad for at least that much. He'd obviously heard Emily. But there was something weird about his speech—not a lisp exactly. He slid over some letters and left the ends off words.

"That's enough!" Ms. Leedy exclaimed. Amelia Leedy, Edgewood High's second oldest living teacher, had shrunk to barely five feet, although rumor had it she used to be tall. Other rumors floated around school, like that she'd been Miss Indiana fifty years ago or maybe seventy-five.

Bren had told Jamie that young Amelia had been married to a bomber pilot in World War II, but he got shot down. Amelia refused to believe he was dead so she never got married again, and even after all this time she still lit a candle in her window and set out a glass of apple cider for him at night just in case he found his way home and was thirsty.

Jamie didn't believe half of Bren's tales. But whatever the fate of poor Ms. Leedy, she'd had the bad luck to draw cafeteria detail this week.

"Let's go have a talk, Ed," Ms. Leedy said, taking him by the arm.

Ed jerked his elbow out of her hand, but he went along peacefully.

Zandrea sighed then shuddered. "That kid gives me the creeps."

"Ed's OK," Bren said.

"Yeah?" Tyler laughed. "Maybe you and Special Ed should have your picture taken together for the next yearbook."

"Well," Bren said, her voice light as whipped cream, "if we do, I'll make sure Ed doesn't get his clothes from *your* closet, Tyler."

"Me?" Tyler whined, staring down at his super-baggy pants, with a 3X shirt that hung to his knees. "What's the matter with the way I dress?" He hoisted up his pants, but it was like trying to hike up a rubber band on a toothpick.

Bren put on her sad puppy dog expression and glanced at the crowd. "Anyone want to break the news to Tyler that the skater punk look went out last year?"

On their walk to class, Jamie confided to Bren, "Lunch is so weird, isn't it? I mean, all morning I look forward to it—*not* for the food, of course. Seeing you and Maya and everybody. But when other kids are around, or when I can't find you guys, I'm thinking, *If I can make it through lunch, I can get through anything.*"

Bren raised one eyebrow and gave Jamie a sideways glance. "Not me! If they moved the lunchroom to the mall, *that's* what I'd think heaven's like."

After school, Jamie waited for Bren by their lockers. The hall had almost cleared out by the time she spotted Bren and Zandrea a dozen lockers away.

Bren hollered, "Ready? Set? Shop!"

Inside the mall, they might as well have been on Mars. Jamie hardly ever hung out here. She'd never admit it to Bren and Zandrea, but she wasn't all that hot on shopping. She'd rather rake leaves or bike to the park and smell autumn.

"Oooh! Oooh!" Bren grabbed Zandrea and Jamie by the arms and pulled them to a small shop called Teamworks. "See?" she said, pointing in the window at loud purple T-shirts. "Those are the ones Dad's buying for the Edgewood Dragons!"

"The Dragons?" Zandrea asked.

"Yes! Isn't that a perfect name? That's the Special Olympics team Jamie and I are helping coach. You could volunteer, too, you know, Zandrea."

Zandrea squinted into the window. "Hello? I told you, Bren. No way am I hanging out with those . . . those kids." She turned sideways and stared at the window, so Jamie figured she must be checking out her reflection. "I admire you for doing it—don't get me wrong. But it would freak me out big-time."

Zandrea headed for the escalators. "Bren, let's check out shoe stores! I could use another pair for cheerleading."

Jamie endured stops in the next six stores, where each salesperson greeted Bren by name and with wild enthusiasm. At this rate, Jamie knew she'd never have time to go home and change before the Gnosh.

"Bren," Jamie said, as Bren stuffed her newly purchased denim change purse into the bag with her new green pleather pants.

"Didn't you say you wanted to check out Martinique's department store?"

"Zandrea!" Bren shouted across the boutique, where Zandrea

had just paid for something from the jewelry counter. "Makeup time!"

They scurried to the end of the mall. Bren led them through the maze of counters like a well-trained lab rat.

"Wait!" Zandrea called, stopping at a glass counter displaying dozens of tiny bottles. "Testers," she said, spraying something from a pale blue bottle onto her wrist and sniffing.

She wrinkled her nose and moved to a clear, round bottle. "Try this. I *love* the way this one smells on me. It's different on everybody, you know." She held the bottle out to Jamie. "Wrist," she commanded.

Jamie stuck out her arm and allowed herself to be sprayed. It smelled like Jessica's nail polish remover. "Nice," she lied.

Bren stuck out her arm, wrist up. "OK. Spray me. But you guys have to tell me what it smells like on me. I have *no* sense of smell. Seriously. It's like a family gene missing from our community gene pool. It's so embarrassing. They say the average person can detect ten thousand different smells. Not me!

"Did you know that if someone poured a bottle of Davidoff's Cool Water Woman over home plate at the Conseco Fieldhouse, people in the highest bleachers could smell it—except for me? And don't even talk about animals! I heard that a male silkworm can sniff out a female seven miles away! If we were silkworms, my whole family would be extinct."

Bren sniffed and sniffed and sniffed her wrist. "Nothing! How does it smell?"

"Very alluring," Zandrea assured her.

Jamie still smelled polish remover, but she kept it to herself.

A tall, middle-aged woman with jet-black hair, a pale blue lab coat, and enough makeup on her face to paint the Edgewood, Indiana, town hall, smiled from across the aisle. "Ladies," she called, "could I interest anyone in a makeover?"

"What's she want to make over?" Jamie whispered.

"You've never had a makeover?" Zandrea accused.

"Jamie Chandler, are you ready to discover your inner diva?" Bren exclaimed, dragging Jamie over to the lady's counter and shoving her onto the stool.

"Jamie, is it?" the makeup lady asked, frowning, studying Jamie's face from all angles.

"Uh huh," Jamie said, her stomach growling. She felt like the backwoods yahoo visiting her city cousins.

"First," said the lady, whose tag read Mona, "let's take off all your makeup with this cleanser. Do you have a good cleanser you prefer, Janie?"

"It's Jamie," Jamie said, shaking her head. Not only didn't she have a good cleanser, but she wasn't wearing any makeup to cleanse.

"Your features are just adorable!" Mona exclaimed, dabbing at Jamie's nose, cheeks, forehead, and chin, while Zandrea and Bren looked on as if they were apprenticed. "You owe it to yourself to make the most of your face."

"That is so true," Zandrea said, frowning.

"What type of skin do you have, Janie?" Mona asked.

"What type?" Jamie repeated. *Type A, like personality? Blood type, like O positive?*

"Oily, dry, flaky . . . ?" Bren offered.

"Um . . ." Jamie thought about it. Sometimes she did get that zit right in the middle of her forehead. And the one on her chin. "Oily, I guess."

"Wrong," Mona said, disappointed. "See what I'm using here?" She looked to Bren and Zandrea for approval. "Astringent. You can already see the difference, can't you? You actually have normal skin. Now, after this, you need to exfoliate before we add moisturizer."

Jamie tried to remember if that's what snakes did when they lost their skins—exfoliated. She closed her eyes while cold grease, squishy creams, and skin-tingly liquids were smeared, splashed, and wiped on her face, to the approving *mmm's* of onlookers.

"Now," Mona said, eyeing Jamie as if she were raw clay to be turned into a sculpture. "Let's make up your palette."

While Mona held up every color to Jamie's face, gathering little bottles and boxes and tubes, Jamie imagined herself sculpting for real. In fact, that's what she'd planned to do before the mall invitation.

For the past several weekends, she'd been experimenting with clay on the garage workbench, molding a rib cage. It still didn't compare with oil or acrylic painting, but an artist had to develop herself in all mediums.

"And after the foundation," Mona was saying, "apply blush

with upward strokes. With this eye cream, you can hide those tiny wrinkles and crow's-feet."

"Wrinkles?" Jamie asked. "I'm fifteen!"

The thick makeup brush tickled her cheeks, and Jamie sneezed.

"That's all right. Our eyeliner and mascara are smudge-proof and water resistant." Mona smudged something on Jamie's eyelids. "You just need to bring out those big blue eyes with earthy greens, like our Eye Enhancers. Dab a metallic shadow on the outer corners. Metallic is huge this fall!

"I would kill for luscious lips like these!" Mona exclaimed, caking on what felt like wax. The pencil tickled her lips, but Jamie tried to keep from twitching. "Lip seal . . . so your boyfriend won't kiss away your lovely lipstick."

"There!" Mona cried, turning Jamie to face her friends. "The all new Janie!"

"You are hot!" Zandrea exclaimed. "Jamie, you've got to get this stuff." Zandrea fingered through the tubes and gels and cleansers and eyeliners Mona had set aside.

"Outstanding! You are *so* fashion forward!" Bren agreed.

Jamie wheeled around to look at the mirror Mona held up proudly. She blinked. She really did look good and at least two years older.

If this is what it takes to be normal, so be it!

Mona rang up the tools of her trade, setting each box carefully into a big white box. "And you get the cosmetic bag with three ounces of cologne for free with your purchase," Mona explained.

"That is *such* a great deal, Jamie!" Zandrea said.

It *was* a great deal, Jamie decided.

Then Mona hit *total.*

Jamie tried not to gag as she stared at the numbers. Slowly, she wrote out a check for just over a month's salary at the Gnosh. She had saved that money for new art supplies.

She ripped off the check, showed her learner's permit as ID, and tried to swallow whatever was trying to rise from her stomach. *I feel like driving the porcelain bus.*

But I had to do this, she told herself. *It will all be worth it.*

By the time Zandrea drove to Jamie's house, Jamie was laughing so hard, she already felt better about the money. Bren had gone into a whole shtick about how she and Zandrea would introduce the new made-over Jamie as "Janie the Great."

"Guys will be dogfighting over you, Janie!" Bren claimed.

Zandrea turned off the engine of her dad's Volvo and got out when Jamie did. "Can I use your bathroom while you change?"

Jamie walked up the sidewalk between Edgewood's two most popular cheerleaders. She felt proud to be part of their circle. She hoped Jessica was home to see it.

Jamie reached for the doorknob. Before she turned it, she thought she heard shouting. She opened the door, hoping it was just the TV.

"Jordan!" Mom yelled down the hallway, her back to Jamie and her friends. "You're being ridiculous!"

Please Reply!

"I mean it!" Jordan screamed from the other end of the hall. "If you don't take these braces off this minute, I'm jumping out of my window! I'm not kidding! Here I go! Good-bye, cruel world. You won't have Jordan Chandler around to laugh at anymore!"

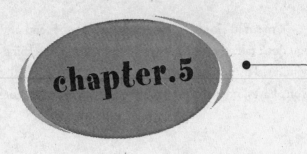

chapter.5

Jordan flung open the door to her bedroom. "I'm jumping!"

Bren's eyes grew as wide as pompoms. "Jordan, no! Mrs. Chandler! Stop her!"

Jordan's door slammed.

Jamie's mother sighed and joined Bren, Zandrea, and Jamie. "Bren, this is a one-story ranch. Jordan won't find a window worth jumping out in the whole house."

Totally embarrassed, Jamie shuffled her friends to the kitchen and asked Mom to get out pretzels for them. Then she raced to her room and changed as fast as she could, careful not to smudge her makeup. Mom had been so preoccupied with Jordan, she hadn't seemed to notice the new Jamie.

But Jessica noticed. "Why is your face so shiny?" Jess asked, trailing Jamie around her bedroom.

"It's makeup, silly," Jamie said, trying to remember if the blue shirt she held in her hands belonged on her color wheel.

Jessica climbed onto Jamie's bed and jumped, her little body hardly wrinkling the bedspread. "I like your old face better," she said.

Time flew at the Gnosh, with customers coming in Friday night waves. Maya flipped over Jamie's new look. She and Morgan helped take orders, while Mrs. Cross joined her husband in the kitchen. Still, Jamie didn't have a down minute all night.

"Man! I can't believe your face is still on!" Maya said after they'd finished mopping the floors and wiping tables. "You got the good stuff, huh? Come on. Let's blow this firetrap. Mr. Beep and I will drive you."

Maya talked makeup to Jamie the whole way, right up to the minute Jamie got out of the car.

"Thanks for the ride," Jamie called, jogging up the walk and dashing straight to her room.

After scrubbing off the makeup, Jamie felt like crashing. But she didn't want to miss the scheduled chat at TodaysGirls.com. She flipped on her computer, waited for it to warm up, and went straight to their Web site and logged on. She greeted everyone, but her mind was moving too slowly to keep up with the cyber banter.

TX2step: u still here, rembrandt?

nycbutterfly: yeah. ur so quiet 2nite! r u going 2B 2kewl
4 us now that ur glamorous???

rembrandt: LOL! sorry. at least i showed. where's Bren?

faithful1: duh! w/ Chad. guys, i've G2G. killer headache!
CYAL8R!

rembrandt: sorry, amber! i've G2G 2. i'm pooped!

jellybean: better go 2 bed! u r going 2 need ur energy
for Special Olympics 2morrow! BTW, mom said i can
help 2! but just 4 tomorrow. if i get good grades this
term, i can b a regular volunteer like u & chic!!!

Jamie had forgotten all about Special Olympics practice. She
wished Bren hadn't forced her into volunteering.

Logging off early, Jamie took a long, hot bath, then got ready
for bed. By the time she'd ransacked through all her cosmetic pur-
chases, found the night cream, and put everything away, it was
nearly midnight.

When Jamie opened her eyes, sunlight streaked through her room.
Jessica was standing next to the bed, so close Jamie could smell morning breath. She groaned and stretched. "What time is it, Jessica?"

"Time for us to go to the Y!" Jessica said, much louder than she
needed to.

"Us?" Jamie sat up in bed. She'd left her window open a crack,
and the smell of green walnuts drifted in on icy air.

Jess ran from the room, yelling, "Mom! Jamie's up!"

A minute later, Mom stuck her head in. "Ms. Reynolds called me into the office, Jamie. That woman acts like I'm her personal slave."

Mom sneezed, then glanced at the ceiling. Jamie wondered if she'd shot up a prayer. Mom was as good as Amber about praying on the spot.

Sighing, Mom said, "I guess I should be thankful for the overtime. We can sure use it. And Jordan's spending the day at Melissa's. Do you mind taking Jessica with you?"

They piled into the car, with Jamie riding shotgun. Mom dropped stone-silent Jordan at her friend's house, then drove Jamie and Jessica to the Y.

"Won't this be great?" Jessica babbled as they buzzed themselves through to the locker rooms. "Did you know they have a district contest next Saturday? And they have to do really good or they can't go to State, which is so much fun!"

Before Jamie could ask her sister how she knew so much about Special Olympics, Jess had run ahead through the locker room and out to the pool.

Jamie had worn her swimsuit under her sweats. She took off her shoes and sweatshirt and stuffed them into an open locker.

"Jamie!" Morgan called when Jamie walked out of the locker room. Morgan ambled up, her bare feet slapping the concrete deck. Although two years younger than her big sis, Morgan had an inch and maybe fifteen pounds on Maya.

Morgan obviously didn't feel the same way Jordan did about braces because nobody smiled more than Morgan.

"Hey, Morgan," Jamie said, glancing around for Jessica.

"This is great! I wish—" Morgan was cut off by a tackle, actually a hug to her knees.

A skinny kid, shorter than Jessica, with bushy brown hair, refused to let go of Morgan's legs.

Struggling to keep her balance, Morgan reached down and patted his head. "Jamie, this is Robbie."

"Swim?" Robbie said, his voice an unnatural pitch, more like a note in a song. "Swim?" he asked again.

"You bet!" Morgan said, waving to Jamie and shuffling poolside, Robbie still attached.

Jamie scanned the deck. Half a dozen girls stood around the diving board, their laughter echoing around the pool.

It struck Jamie that these swimmers came in all sizes. Sure, on the high school team, Maya was kind of short, and Bren tall. Anastasia, the backup butterfly, was 5'10".

But compared to this Special Olympics team, the high school swimmers looked like factory cut-outs. One guy standing by himself looked way over six feet. Another one sitting on the bleachers, a purple towel around his shoulders, must have weighed 250 pounds. Then there was Morgan's Robbie, who couldn't have stretched to more than four feet on tiptoes.

Jamie spotted Bren at the far side of the pool, surrounded by swimmers.

"First time?" came a deep voice that startled her.

Jamie turned to see Alan Snyder, Edgewood High's sure winner of valedictorian this year. "Alan?"

"You're in for a good time," he said, snapping his head back to sling his wet black hair out of his chocolate brown eyes.

"Guaranteed. This is my third year helping with swimming. Last spring I coached basketball. It was sweet! Mrs. Pearson's a great swim coach. Do you know her?"

Jamie saw Mrs. Pearson coming toward them. "She goes to our church."

"Great!" Alan called to Mrs. Pearson, "I'll get them lined up!" Then he walked to the bleachers and began calling out names.

"Thanks for coming, Jamie!" Mrs. Pearson said, juggling her clipboard in a way that reminded Jamie of Harry. "I really want the kids to do well at district. I'd love to see some of them go on to State."

Jamie smiled weakly. "I—I'm not sure I know what to do."

"Help them swim better," she said, blowing her whistle at the diving-board crowd. "Be their friend."

Bren came running up, slowing down when one of the kids hollered "No running!" at her.

"Isn't this amazing!" Bren exclaimed. "Some of these kids could swim on our team, easy! Wait 'til you meet Leslie and Sandy!"

As if on cue, Sandy walked up. She was about Bren's size, with auburn hair that fell in ringlets. Sandy stopped close to Bren and ran her fingers through Bren's hair.

"There you are!" squealed Bren. "We were just talking about

you!" Sandy had a smile that took up her whole face, and Jamie found herself grinning, too, in spite of her nervousness.

Everyone took a seat on the bleachers, and Alan told them to listen up to the coach. As Mrs. Pearson introduced volunteers and explained details about the district meet, several of the kids scooted down rows of bleachers to sit by Jamie and Bren.

One girl, who took the seat right next to Jamie, had the greenest eyes Jamie had ever seen, wide-set and huge, as if she were continually surprised by everything around her. With her dark hair and angular features, she could have been a fashion model.

It was only when they all stood up to move to the water that Jamie noticed how stiffly the girl walked, as if an invisible coat hanger held neck, back, and arms separate from her body.

Bren jumped right into the pool with the girls, while Morgan took her time on the steps, urged on by splashing swimmers.

Jamie wasn't sure which way to go. She started to follow Morgan, then remembered Jessica. Panic dug into her chest, and she felt as if someone had knocked the wind out of her. Her mind burst into flashbacks of Jessica's Gnosh disappearance. She glanced furtively around the deck.

There was Jessica, sitting at the opposite end of the pool, legs dangling in the water. She was watching as some guy swam to the bottom, then burst to the surface, splashing her and sending her into convulsions of laughter.

Thanks, God, Jamie prayed, angry with herself for forgetting to ask for help when she'd panicked.

It really made no sense. She always felt an amazing peace come rushing in whenever she did finally turn to God. But she kept forgetting He was there for her.

"Jess! Come here!" she shouted.

A dozen heads turned toward her, but Jessica's wasn't one of them.

"Jess!"

Irritated that she had to go get her little sister, Jamie stormed to the other end of the pool. "Jessica, I—"

"Jamie!" Jessica exclaimed. "This is my friend from church, the one I told you about? Eddy!"

Jamie forced a smile and nodded at the guy in the pool. He wasn't half bad looking.

But he looked familiar. Jamie did a double take. "Ed?" It was Ed from school. Special Ed. *This* was Jess's Eddy? But he looked so different here.

"Eddy is the team's best swimmer," Jessica explained. "He's going to smoke everybody at district! That's what that boy over there said." Jessica pointed to one of the boys swimming in the lane.

"I better go," Ed said. He swam to the other side, where Mrs. Pearson was giving instructions.

Jamie watched Ed's clean, smooth strokes. When he reached the side, guys gathered around him, elbowing each other out of the way so they could stand next to Ed. He said something to Robbie, who had been screaming, and Robbie quieted down.

The rest of practice, while the good swimmers did time trials, Jamie and Bren helped Sandy and Leslie try to float on their backs. Leslie reminded Jamie of a black-haired Tinkerbell, tall and thin with short hair. But something was wrong with one of Leslie's arms. Her left arm ended in a fist with no fingers and hung at her side about half the length of her right arm. She and Sandy laughed through the whole lesson, even though Leslie couldn't help sinking.

Finally, Jamie got Sandy to relax in her arms and lie back on top of the water. Sandy's auburn ringlets spread around her head and over Jamie's arm. Then slowly, Jamie slid her arms away, allowing the unsuspecting Sandy to float on her back for the first time in her life—for ten whole seconds.

"Sandy," Jamie said, holding her hands up out of the water. "Look! No hands. You're floating, girl!"

Immediately, Sandy sank like an anchor. She came up, coughing and spitting out water. "I did it!" she cried. "Did you see me? I floated!"

"I saw!" Bren shouted. "You rock!"

"Yea, Sandy!" Leslie yelled, sounding more excited for Sandy than Sandy was herself.

Leslie made a one-arm climb out of the pool and speed-walked to Mrs. Pearson's group. "Sandy floated! Sandy can float on her back!"

Ed was the first to stop swimming. "Way to go, Sandy!" he shouted, as if she'd just won the Olympic gold.

Ed wasn't the only one. Soon everybody got out of the water to congratulate Sandy. Jessica joined in, leaning over so far to give Sandy a high-five that Jamie was afraid she'd fall in.

It took several minutes to get swimmers back to their marks. Then Mrs. Pearson called Bren and Jamie over to the side. "I have a favor to ask," she said. "We don't have anybody signed up to swim backstroke. I just haven't had time to work on it yet. The only swimmer I think could handle it in such a short time is Ed . . . and maybe Darren . . . or Tina. Would you get them started on the basics?"

Bren answered yes for both of them. "Let's work on-deck first, like Coach did with us," Bren suggested. "Remember? I'll walk them through the movements."

Jamie was glad to have Bren take over. She couldn't imagine teaching Ed the backstroke.

Darren, Ed, and Tina, a dark-eyed, thin girl Jamie judged to be about her age, clustered around Bren. Jamie tried hard to get all the names straight, but there were just so many of them.

"I *love* the backstroke!" Bren exclaimed. "I don't usually get to compete in our meets. But if I do, it's in backstroke. Who says it's normal to swim on our tummies? I mean, look at fish. Do they even *have* a tummy? Well, now that you mention it, I suppose whales and dolphins—"

"Bren!" Jamie whispered, giving her friend the *get-on-with-it* glare.

Jessica, who had sneaked up behind Eddy, giggled.

"Oops!" Bren said. "Where were we?"

"YMCA!" Darren answered.

Bren laughed. "Thanks, Darren. I better keep you around."

"Me too," Tina said.

"OK. You know Jamie, right?" Bren grabbed Jamie's wrist and pulled her front and center.

Jamie felt her cheeks flush. Her mouth twitched into a nervous smile.

"Jamie," Bren announced, "will lie on her back now and demonstrate—"

"Bren!" Jamie felt like a trained seal at Water-rama.

"—and demonstrate the backstroke while the rest of us stand around her and do the same movements," Bren finished. She stared at Jamie, waiting, leaving nothing for her to do but lie down on the cold deck.

Jamie shivered when her bare back met damp concrete.

Tina laughed. "It's cold!"

"Yup," Jamie said, stretching out, feeling water from the wet deck seep into her suit. "Get on with it, Bren!"

"Now the rest of you follow along standing up while Jamie shows the motions," Bren instructed. "Arms to your sides. Legs together!"

Jamie obeyed, her legs sloshing concrete sludge as she pulled them together. Above her, she heard hands slapping thighs and feet shuffling.

"You guys rock!" Bren exclaimed. "Now slide your hands up your sides. Then fling them up, out, and *down!* Everybody! Up! Out! Down!"

Jamie moved her arms in the backstroke, scooping up wetness and who-knew-what-else as she swept the deck. She wished she were standing up like the rest of them, instead of lying in pool deck gunk.

"What about our legs?" Ed asked.

"Legs?" Bren sounded as if she'd never considered those appendages. "Ah, legs! Thanks, Ed. Wouldn't want to forget our legs! Let's see . . . Up . . ."

Jamie heard chuckles and rolled over on her side to peek at Bren. Bren's forehead wrinkled with concentration as she lifted both arms and one leg.

"Up . . . ," she said. "Up with everything, I guess. Arms *and* legs." Bren stood on one leg, looking like a flamingo.

"Then it's . . . ," Bren muttered to herself, flailing her arms to keep her balance. "Up, out, together . . . No, wait! That's not it. Let me start over."

Jamie risked a glance at Ed. He had his hand over his mouth, but his eyes were laughing. Tina laughed out loud.

Darren frowned. "That looks hard," he said.

"No way, Darren!" Bren said. "It's really—"

Jamie saw it happening, but she was too late to do anything about it. Bren's left foot caught her right ankle just as she said "—easy!"

Bren's arms waved. She hopped on one foot, then lost her balance and toppled sideways.

Ed rushed in to make the save, grabbing Bren around the waist an instant before her head would have cracked concrete.

"Yea, Ed!" Darren shouted.

"Way to go, Eddy!" Jessica screamed. "You saved Bren!"

Bren stumbled to her feet. "I owe you big-time. Thanks!"

Practice ended and the swimmers headed for the lockers—except Ed. He dived back in and started laps.

Jamie looked around for Jessica and saw her making her way over to Eddy in the far lane. "Jessica, let's go!" she shouted.

Jessica didn't bother turning around.

"Jess, I mean it! Now!"

Morgan walked by on her way to the locker room. "Jessica doesn't want to go home, huh? She was so good though, wasn't she?"

"Until now," Jamie said. "Jess!" she yelled again. "Morgan, tell Bren we'll be right in."

Morgan grabbed her towel off the bleachers and tossed Jamie's to her. "Good luck," she said, padding away.

Mrs. Pearson and one of the mothers seemed to be in deep conversation high in the bleachers. The only others left in the pool area were Ed, Jessica, and Jamie.

Jamie tried one more time, her anger growing. "Jessica Chandler, come here right now!"

Jessica didn't budge. *Now I know how her teacher feels!* Jamie fumed as she walked the long way around to her sister.

"Jessica! What is with you?" she shouted, only a few feet away now.

Still Jessica refused to answer. Jamie stormed up and took Jessica's elbow, lifting her out of her cross-legged squat. "It's time to go!"

Jessica turned her green eyes on Jamie. "Sorry, Jamie."

Jamie's anger dissolved instantly. She could never stay mad at Jess. "Well, get on in the locker room and dry off. And listen from now on, Jess."

Jessica darted off, leaving her towel behind.

"Jess! Your towel!" Jamie called after her.

Jessica kept going.

Jamie picked up the towel and shook her head. "That kid," she muttered. She sensed Ed watching her from the pool and turned to look. He was holding on to the side of the pool, just a foot from her.

Jamie felt she should say something to him. But what? *Hey, Ed, you're not as weird as I thought?*

Great, Jamie thought, giving up. *I'm as good at conversation here as I am everywhere else.*

"Your sister," Ed said. "She doesn't hear right."

Jamie turned and frowned at him. "What did you say?"

"Jessica," he answered, his voice soft but firm. "There's something wrong."

"What are you talking about?" Jamie heard the edge in her voice. She couldn't help it. Something was tightening in her chest, making it hard to squeeze out words.

"Something's wrong with Jessica's hearing," Ed said. "Jamie, your sister needs a doctor."

chapter.6

Jamie watched Ed dive under water and swim away. But his words echoed in her ears: *Something's wrong with Jessica's hearing. Your sister needs a doctor.*

"Ed!" Jamie shouted. "You're wrong!" She tried to laugh. *No way! Jessica is the most normal kid in the world.*

Ed reached the end of the pool, pulled himself out, and walked to the locker room.

"Ed! I'm talking to—" *Of course!* Jamie thought. *Ed can't hear me. He's the one with bad hearing. He probably thinks everybody has hearing problems.* She took a deep breath. *That had to be it.*

A flashback lurked in the corners of Jamie's mind—Jamie screaming at Jess, who sits cross-legged a few feet away, never once flinching. And another—Jamie trying to get Jess to take a glass of orange juice, but Jessica talking on and on about socks as if she doesn't—

So what? Jamie told herself, heading to the lockers. *Anyone can see how normal Jess is just by looking at her.*

Jamie charged into the locker room.

"Jamie!" Bren shouted. "Over here!"

"I have to go," Jamie said, looking around for Jessica.

"But Maya's coming to pick us up," Bren said. "She and Amber are going to the mall, and they thought we—"

"Can't," Jamie said.

Jessica was sitting on one of the wooden benches, putting on her tennis shoes.

Jamie put her hand on Jessica's shoulder. "Come on, Jess. We'll walk home."

"But what about—?" Bren's voice sounded whiny.

"Bye, Bren," Jamie called, not glancing back. "Later."

The sun on her back felt good as Jamie walked north past the courthouse, with Jessica at her side, running to keep up. A minty pine scent blew in the crisp wind that made Jessica's nylon jacket bubble with air.

This is stupid! Jamie thought. *It's like I'm scared to talk to my own sister.*

"Are you mad at me?" Jessica asked as they crossed the street to cut through the park.

Jamie turned and gazed at Jessica's upturned face, her hair tucked under a Cleveland Indian cap. "No, Jess. Of course I'm not mad at you."

Jessica shrugged.

Jamie realized her fingernails were cutting into the palms of her clenched fists. Somehow it reminded her to pray: *Help me out here, God.*

"Jess?" Jamie knew she was shouting. "Things any better at school?"

Jessica shrugged again, her little shoulders making her jacket rustle.

Can she hear me? Jamie wondered.

"I like school pretty much," Jessica said. "I don't know what I'm doing to make my teacher mad. I try to pay attention, Jamie. Honest! Sometimes I just miss stuff."

Jamie loved her sister's voice. She lowered her own voice and asked softly, "Jessica, could you be having trouble hearing?"

Jessica squinted up at her. "What?"

Jamie felt hot tears burn her throat. It all made sense—Jessica not coming in at recess when the whistle blew, not doing assignments. No wonder Jess had misunderstood her at the Gnosh and gone home alone. She hadn't heard right.

A dog barked from someone's backyard. Overhead on a telephone wire, an oriole chittered. A car door slammed somewhere. Somebody laughed.

And my sister can't hear any of it.

Jamie shut herself up with her computer the rest of the day. She needed answers, and she needed them **now!**

Jess will be fine, she told herself as she waited for her screen to blink on and systems to load. Impatient, she tried to connect to the Internet before her dinosaur computer had fully awakened. It didn't work.

She waited, tapping her foot on the worn blue carpet, staring around at the poster art that covered her walls. This year Joan Miró had held her imagination. His bright primary colors splashed wiry black squiggles that could alternately depress or cheer her. Now Jamie stared at one of Miró's moon-faced outlines and felt like crying over it.

Finally her temperamental server let her enter cyberspace, and she clicked onto one of the search engines that let users refine their searches when too many hits pop up.

She typed into the Search box: "hearing."

It took forever, but at last page one of a long list of 2,556 hits came into focus.

She clicked on Search These Results and typed in: "loss."

Better. She still had over a hundred sites listed, but the first few sounded like what she wanted. Following the trail of "hearing loss—common causes," she landed on a list of articles in newspaper format. Jamie called up the article titled, "Common Hearing Loss in Children."

Heart pounding, she read the first paragraph:

While there may be numerous causes of hearing loss in young children, the number one reason for insufficient

hearing is a cold or infection. Recent studies reveal that as many as 1 out of 3 children may suffer temporary hearing loss due to simple or chronic ear infections, normally in children susceptible to the common cold.

"Yes!" Jamie exclaimed out loud. *One out of three! Common. Simple. Normal!*

The article went on to suggest that although many colds and infections, along with related problems, clear up all by themselves, it's always a good idea to consult your family physician.

Jamie reread the line about problems clearing up by themselves. *That's what will happen with Jessica,* she told herself. *I'm positive.*

The answer had come more easily than she'd expected. Jamie leaned back in her chair, relief blowing over her like the autumn air from her open window. She'd known it all along, really. Jessica's hearing would be back to normal in no time flat.

Until then, Jamie would cover for her little sister. *No sense getting Mom upset over nothing. She has enough on her hands with the new law partner. Besides, Jessica doesn't need anything to worry about. She'll be fine.*

Mom had gone all out for dinner. Jamie smelled lasagna and garlic bread all the way from her room.

"Cool! I'm starved!" Jamie said, filling the water glasses.

"You sound better," Mom said. She set a big bowl of salad in the middle of the table. "Did Special Olympics practice wear you out?"

"Something like that." Jamie took her seat between Jordan and Jessica, across from Mom's place.

"Jessica told me she had fun at the Y," Mom said, sitting down, then popping right back up. "Forgot the dressing." She got a bottle of Italian from the fridge door. "What's your friend's name, Jess? That boy from church who swims on the team?"

Jessica didn't answer.

"Ed!" Jamie answered for her. "Eddy Spenser."

Jordan frowned at Jamie, and she knew she was shouting.

"Eddy swims for the Special Olympics team," Jess said.

"So you've said." Mom sat down and scooted her chair in.

Jamie couldn't help wondering if Jessica had heard the squeak of chair leg on linoleum. Mom reached out and bowed her head. They all held hands while she prayed:

"Father, thank You for Your nearness to us. We know it's because of all Your Son did for us by dying on the cross. We're so grateful."

Jamie opened one eye to peek at Jessica. Jess was staring at Mom's mouth.

". . . and for my girls. Thanks for always taking care of us. Oh—and thank You for our dinner. Amen."

"Amen," Jamie mumbled with Jordan and Jessica as the three of them reached for garlic bread.

Again, Jamie realized that she hadn't been keeping up her conversation with God. Maybe now that she'd resolved Jessica's problem, it would be easier. She took a second to thank God that Jessica's hearing problem was no more serious than the common cold.

"Good bread, Mom," Jordan said, her mouth full. Still, it was more than Jamie had heard out of Jordan for a couple of days. Jordan slammed down her fork and picked at something stuck in her braces. "I hate these things!" she mumbled.

"Great lasagna," Jamie said, the ricotta melting on her tongue.

"Well, it's my way of apologizing," Mom said.

"This is so good, Mom," Jessica said.

"What? Oh thanks, Jess. I was saying . . . I wanted to apologize to you girls for spending so much time at the office lately. I know we can use the overtime, but I still wouldn't have gone back nights if it hadn't been for that new partner."

"Ms. Reynolds, right?" Jamie said, her hand bumping Jordan's as they reached for seconds on garlic bread.

"Right," Mom said, sitting up straighter. "I know I'm *just* a paralegal, and she's brought in all these clients. But I have been there a lot longer than she has. I'm good at what I do, if you'll excuse me for saying so. But that woman acts like I'm nothing, like I should be on call to get her coffee! And heaven help me if I make one tiny mistake—"

"I'd love steak!" Jessica gulped her water and set down the glass. "I haven't had a steak since we cooked out when I was in kindergarten."

Jamie knew Jessica thought Mom said *steak* instead of *mistake*, but Mom and Jordan exchanged baffled looks.

Before Mom could ask, Jamie said quickly, "Yeah, Jess. We all love steak, and it takes lots of overtime to buy it. So we understand where you're coming from, Mom."

"Huh?" Jessica asked.

"Did anybody happen to think of me?" Jordan asked. "I'm not allowed steak! It's not enough punishment that I'm forced to wear a chicken-wire fence in my mouth, to talk like Daffy Duck, to set off metal detectors in airports. No! They won't let me eat anything good—no steak, no popcorn—"

"Jordan, that's not fair," Mom said. "Those braces are part of the reason I even consider overtime. The least you could do is . . ."

Grateful for the distraction, even in the form of an argument, Jamie winked at Jessica.

Close call.

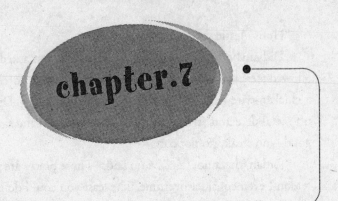

chapter.7

Later that night when Jamie logged on to TodaysGirls.com, the first thing that greeted her was Amber's Thought for the Day. She'd added Exodus 4:10–11 below the Psalm 139 verse about being fearfully and wonderfully made.

But Moses said to the Lord, "But Lord, I am not a skilled speaker. I have never been able to speak well. . . . I speak slowly and can't find the best words."
Then the Lord said to him, "Who made man's mouth? And who makes him deaf or not able to speak?"

Jamie shuddered. Amber had picked a verse about being deaf? It was eerie how often Amber's verses struck a deep chord in Jamie's own life. She would check out Amber's Thought for the Day and feel as if Amber had read her mind. But Amber would be the first one to admit *she* couldn't read minds. That was God's business— reading minds and knowing hearts.

Amber's Thought for the Day, under the verse, read:

Don't forget! God made ALL of you, your whole person! And He still says you're cool. So if you disagree, you'll have to take it up with God!

I'm being stupid all over again, Jamie told herself. *Nothing's wrong with Jessica's hearing—or there won't be, once her infection clears up. I'm the one who can't speak well.*

Jamie clicked into their chat room and logged on. Maya and Morgan were at it again. Jamie hardly ever saw them argue in person, except when Maya got too bossy, or Morgan failed to live up to her big sister's fashion standards. The Cross family was about as normal as a family could get.

nycbutterfly: u still should have asked!! i don't borrow UR clothes do i????
jellybean: u hate all my clothes
nycbutterfly: Y would u ruin my sweater??!!!!
jellybean: sorry!! forgot the M&M's were in the pockets.
TX2step: Y do U 2 fight here??? fight on ur own time!! BD--just a sweater

nycbutterfly: just???!!! faithful1--u settle this. should my sis buy me a new sweater?

faithful1: Whoa!! im neutral!

chicChick: which country is supposed 2B neutral all the time?

Jamie actually knew the answer to that one. She typed in:

rembrandt: Hey! Switzerland is neutral.

chicChick: WB, rembrandt! Switzerland? They make those knives, right? Swiss army knives? U No, if those R the weapons of choice for the Swiss army, no wonder they r neutral! They r so CUTE--did u no they have scissors and nail files and toothpicks . . .

Chat went on for over an hour, and Jamie forgot about everything else. She laughed as Bren and Maya discussed their current boyfriends. Bren had devised a new rating system for guys and dates, based on 21 points—pure Bren logic.

Alex had just received a letter from her mother. Alex was living with her Indiana grandparents while her parents sorted out their lives in Texas. Jamie knew that rough, tough Alex missed her parents more than she'd admit.

Amber chatted about her history paper and how tough her teacher graded. But Jamie knew Amber would end up with an A+. She always did.

Before going to bed, Jamie crossed the hall to the room Jordan and Jessica shared. Mom had gone to bed early, so the house seemed unnaturally silent. Easing the door open, Jamie found Jordan at her desk, flipping through a teen magazine, her head bobbing to music only she could hear through her headphones.

Jamie waved at her, then crossed the room to Jessica's bed. Jess's black hair spread over the pillow, and her tiny mouth turned up in a crooked grin.

Only Jess would smile in her sleep, Jamie thought. *Maybe tomorrow she'll wake up and the ear infection will be gone.*

Jamie felt a pang of guilt for not confiding in Mom. What would be wrong in telling Mom Jess needed to see a doctor for her ear infection? If Mom believed Jess was in any kind of pain, she'd take her to the hospital immediately.

But Jess isn't in pain. And most infections clear up by themselves. And everything will go back to normal for her.

Still, Jamie thought as she climbed into her own bed, *why haven't I told Mom?*

Because you're afraid, answered a little voice deep inside of her.

But there was nothing to be afraid of. True, she *had* been afraid before she got her answer off the Internet. Not now though.

Still, Jamie couldn't shut out the little voice so easily. *You're afraid a doctor might find something else, something more serious than an infection. You're afraid they'll say Jessica's hearing isn't normal. She's like Ed.*

Jamie pulled the pillow over her head. She had to stop thinking like that. *Dear God,* she prayed, *clear up Jessica's ear infection. Make her hearing normal again—fast!*

The next morning when Jessica yelled, "Jamie! Wake up! Time for church," Jamie felt as if she'd barely dozed off.

"It can't be morning," she groaned.

Jessica pulled back the covers. "We leave in thirty minutes. Even Jordan's dressed."

"I heard that!" Jordan hollered from the hallway.

Suddenly Jamie remembered why she hadn't gotten a good night's sleep. Maybe God had answered her prayer, and Jessica's ears were back to normal.

Jamie decided to experiment while she had Jessica to herself. "Jess?" she shouted as Jessica headed for the doorway.

Jessica turned around. "Huh?"

"Want to ride in the front seat?" she whispered.

Last month, even last week, Jessica would have jumped at the invitation. Jamie always rode shotgun on Sundays.

"Did you want something?" Jessica asked.

Too soft, Jamie reasoned. *I could barely hear myself.* She sat up in bed and tried again, a little louder. "Do you want to ride in the front seat today?"

Jessica frowned, as if looking harder would make her hear better. "Why did I eat today? You mean pancakes?"

Jamie felt tears swell behind her eyes. She willed them away. *Why are you taking so long to answer, God?* she prayed.

"Nothing, Jess," she said. "Go on. I'll be out."

When Jamie spotted Harry and his boys on the church steps, she felt as if she hadn't seen him for weeks. Nat and Harry Jr. were swinging on the railing, while Mrs. Short chased after Chris, their youngest.

"There's my newest swimmer and former assistant!" Harry said as Jamie joined them on the steps.

Jamie reached over the railing and pulled up Nat, who was dangling from the bottom railing while his brother laughed.

"Careful, guys," she said, setting Nat on his feet.

Turning to Harry, Jamie was overcome with the urge to confide in him, to tell him everything about Jessica. He'd know the right thing to do. He'd understand why she'd held it in this long. "Harry—" she began.

The bells sounded from the spire at the front of the sanctuary. Harry gathered the boys and began herding them inside. "Go sit by your mother," he commanded. He smiled over his shoulder at Jamie. "What's up?"

Latecomers scurried past them. Inside, the song leader asked everyone to rise, and creaking and shuffling could be heard as the congregation stood.

"Never mind," she said. "We better go in."

Jamie's family occupied the pew behind the Thomases. Amber and her brother sat on either side of their mother during the service. Morgan, who usually rode to church with Amber, sat with them. Jamie knew Amber's dad traveled a lot for his trucking business, so he didn't always make it.

Morgan turned, smiled at Jamie, and then seemed to zero in on the sermon the rest of the hour.

Jamie tried to concentrate, but all she could think of was Jessica. Could Jess even hear the sermon?

Then something the pastor said caught Jamie's attention: "Most of us have something we don't like about ourselves."

Been there, Jamie thought. *Who am I kidding? I AM there.*

"Admit it," he said, leaning his elbows on the podium. "Isn't there at least one thing you hate about yourself?"

Jamie considered that. *Alphabetized or in order of hatred?*

"Maybe you hate your nose. Or perhaps no matter how hard you try, you can't do the things that seem so easy for those around you. You can't quite fit in."

He had her now. That was how Jamie felt most of the time. Amber and Bren never had trouble talking to other kids or saying funny things or being part of any group. And nobody had to work as many hours or baby-sit as much as Jamie did.

"Turn in your Bibles to second Corinthians, chapter twelve, starting at verse nine: "'When you are weak, then my power is made perfect in you.' So I am very happy to brag about my weaknesses. Then Christ's power can live in me. So I am happy when I have weaknesses . . . because when I am weak, then I am truly strong.'"

Jamie followed along, but the verses made no sense. *Brag about weaknesses?* She smiled to herself. *Right! Look at me, everybody! I never know what to say to people! You should see me try to say clever things! Oh, and look—no dad!*

Jamie believed all the stuff in the Bible was true. But this one—being happy about weaknesses—was a stretch.

After church Mom stayed to meet with a couple of people about the food bank the church ran for the community. Jordan, who hadn't opened her mouth, even to sing, retreated to the car. Jessica and Ed ran outside, and Jamie watched them throw a paper-bulletin airplane back and forth by the parking lot.

Jamie hung out on the lawn with Morgan. She was listening to Morgan's story about one of the kids at Special Olympics, when she heard Ed shout:

"Jessica! No!"

Jamie's heart froze. Jess was running toward the street. She was laughing, chasing the paper airplane.

"Stop her!" someone cried.

"No!" screamed a man's voice.

Then half a dozen voices yelled Jessica's name as Jamie raced toward the street, faster and faster, colors blurring, her legs moving by themselves.

Jessica, seemingly oblivious to the cries for her to stop, heedless of everything except the renegade paper airplane, jogged down the ditch and up the other side. Her little body moved fast and steady—and straight into the street as a car sped around the corner.

"Got it!" Jessica yelled.

Jamie saw everything in slow motion as she reached the ditch. The car got closer. Brakes screeched. Jessica turned. Her mouth flew open. She cried out, eyes as wide as tires. The car, unable to stop, swerved, came closer, skidding sideways, heading straight for Jessica.

chapter.8

N o!" Jamie screamed as she plunged down the ditch. Her toe caught a rock. She tripped, rolling down, down, then thudding to a stop.

Afraid of what she'd see, Jamie made herself look at the road.

Jessica was in someone's arms. Jamie had to squint against the sun to see. *Ed.* Ed was carrying Jessica.

Jamie scrambled to her feet and ran to them. "Is she OK? Are you OK, Jess?" Tears of fear and relief flooded her eyes.

Ed set Jessica down in the grass. A crowd was forming around them, but all Jamie could see was her sister. Jessica was safe.

"Sorry," Jessica said as Jamie wrapped her arms around her. Jess was trembling. "I didn't see the car."

"You're OK, Jessica," Ed said.

"Thanks to you," Jamie managed. She shut her eyes and hugged tighter, needing to smell the peach of Jessica's hair.

Amber, Morgan, and Jordan rushed up at the same time.

"I saw that car heading right for you, you little jerk!" Jordan cried, tears making her choke. "You scared me to death, Jess! I yelled for you to stop. Why didn't you stop?"

"Because she couldn't hear you, Jordan," Jamie said quietly.

Her mother ran up and threw her arms around Jessica. "Are you all right, honey? What on earth happened?"

"It's all my fault," Jamie said. She glanced at Ed, then back at Mom.

"How is it your fault?" Mom asked, not letting go of Jessica.

"Because I knew Jess couldn't hear, and I pretended she was OK."

"Jessica? Jess can't hear? What are you talking about?" Mom stared at Jess as if she could tell by looking at her.

"For a week, Mom, maybe longer," Jamie explained. "She can hear, but not normally. I think that's why she's had trouble in school."

Jamie heard people whispering around them. Somebody was urging everybody to go on home, that it was all over.

"Jessica," Jamie said loudly, making sure her sister was looking directly at her. "I think something's wrong with your hearing. Do you think so?"

Jessica pressed her lips together, then shifted her mouth to the side of her face, a thinking-hard gesture she'd had even as a baby. "I thought everybody was talking real soft," she said.

Jamie hugged her again, pressing Jessica's head to her chest. "I love you, Jess."

Jessica rolled her head back to gaze up at Jamie. "I didn't even know you knew how to play *chess*."

Jess's reply cracked open the door they needed to slip through to laugh, to breathe, to believe everything would be all right again.

Mom thanked Ed a million times, then drove home at about two miles per hour.

Chat that night centered around Jessica.

chicChick: r u sure the li'l sweetie is k?
rembrandt: Jess is fine. my mom is having a hard time tho. blames herself
jellybean: Y??
rembrandt: cuz she didn't figure out sooner that Jess couldn't hear. she sez she would have if she hadn't worked so much
TX2step: it's totally not her fault!

Jamie had spent all afternoon convincing Mom that she wasn't the world's worst mother. But the tension at home felt heavy enough to sink a sub.

faithful1: what R U going 2 do about Jess?
rembrandt: Mom got Doc Wheeler's answering service. She's taking Jess for a checkup 2morrow.

nycbutterfly: i'll bet it's an ear infection. jellybean used
   2 get them all the time.
jellybean: did not!!!
nycbutterfly: did 2!
TX2step: ACK! here we go again!!!

When Jamie signed out of the chat room, she backtracked to Amber's Thought for the Day. Amber had obviously gotten more out of the sermon than Jamie had. She'd posted the verse about weakness making you strong.

Jamie reread the verse: *I am very happy to brag about my weaknesses.* But it didn't make any more sense now than it had in church. *So I'm supposed to brag about being such a loser, so unpopular? Sorry,* she thought. *No matter how much I might brag about being the odd-woman-out in this life, I'd still rather be Bren.*

That night after turning off her bedroom light, Jamie opened her curtains and gazed out at the blue-black sky dotted with white stars. Then she dashed to her bed and snuggled under her big comforter. *Lord,* she prayed, *I just have one request: Please make Jessica completely well again.*

Monday morning Mom phoned the law office to tell them she wouldn't be coming in. Jamie overheard enough of the conversation to make out that Ms. Reynolds herself was on the other end of the line.

"No, I'm not sick," Mom said into the receiver. "I'm taking my daughter to the doctor."

There was a pause. Jamie watched as Mom twisted the cord around her finger.

"I don't suppose it *will* take all day. But I'm still spending it with my daughter."

Pause.

"Listen to me, Ms. Reynolds," Mom said in an icy tone Jamie rarely heard. "I love my job, but I love my family more. Don't make me choose, or you and the firm will lose. Do we understand each other?"

Pause.

Mom winked at Jamie and Jordan. "Why thank you. I'll tell her," Mom said sweetly. "Uh huh. And you have a good day, too."

"Way to go, Mom!" Jamie exclaimed after Mom hung up.

Jordan gave a thumbs-up, accompanied by a closed-lipped grin.

"I want to go with you," Jamie begged. She and Mom had already had this conversation, and Jamie hadn't fared any better than Ms. Reynolds.

"What I need from you," Mom answered, "is prayer. You and Jordan go to school as normal."

The word *normal* echoed in her ears as Jamie ran to Harry's car. Harry and the others grilled her on Jessica all the way to school.

At swim practice, Jamie went through the motions.

"You'll have to do better than that to get off the bench, Chandler," Zandrea said after Jamie turned in her worst time in the breaststroke.

"Don't worry about Jessica," Maya said in the locker room. "She'll be just fine. You'll see!"

What Jamie wanted, what she really needed, was time alone with Harry. But she didn't get it. By the time she got dressed, it was first block.

Somehow Jamie made it to lunch. Bren waited for her, and they zipped through the pizza line. Jamie might as well have ordered cardboard or the dreaded chili con carne. She sat between Bren and Morgan, and she even nibbled up to the crust of her pizza. But she couldn't taste.

Dear God, she prayed. *Take care of Jess. Make the doctor fix whatever's wrong with her ears. Make it be over. And make Jess normal.*

It was the hundredth time she'd put in her request. All around her voices banged together, loud as silverware. The roar of scraping, shouting, laughing, and clanging rose steadily, like static turned louder and louder until she wanted to scream.

"There he is!" Bren cried, elbowing Jamie, bringing her mind back to her body. Bren pointed across the cafeteria to a table where Ed sat alone. "Did he really run right out in front of that car to save Jessica?"

"All I saw was after the save," Amber said. "But Ed's a hero in my book."

Jamie watched the way Ed's eyes darted, taking in the whole cafeteria, warding off attack. Hard to believe this was the same Ed from the Y. *That* Ed never would have had to sit by himself.

"I'm going over there and thank him," she said, pushing away her pizza. Her heart beat as if she were about to run and save *him* from an oncoming car.

"You go, girl!" Bren called after her.

Jamie slid between two tables and across the aisle. One more table and she'd be there.

"Jamie?" Zandrea looked up from her table as Jamie eased in front of it. "Did you bring that metallic shadow?"

"What?" Jamie watched as Ed stepped into the trash line behind Chad.

"Hello? Your eye shadow?" Zandrea demanded.

Jamie looked on as Chad did something to Ed's hair. Ed swiped at the irritation. Chad's buddies chortled, smothering laughs. She might have been bird-watching, observing the mysterious habits of rare species.

"Jamie!" Zandrea sounded disgusted. "Rewind! Hey . . . you're not wearing your makeup! Why . . . ?"

But Jamie ignored Zandrea. She was much too fascinated watching *this* odd species. Ed. *Special Ed,* Chad dubbed him.

"Fine," Zandrea said, smoothing out her caramel suede jacket, brushing crumbs from her animal-print skirt. "I'll find somebody who actually *wears* makeup."

Jamie couldn't take her eyes off Ed's hearing aids. They stuck out larger than life, neon signs announcing: *Look at me! I'm handicapped!*

Why do they tease Ed? Jamie wondered, not budging, even when Zandrea pushed past her. Jamie watched as a freshman snatched Ed's half-eaten cobbler from his tray.

Is it because he can't hear well? What if Jessica's hearing doesn't get better? Then what? Will Jessica join the rank of Ed's "species"? And if they treat Ed like this, what will they do to Jess?

Jamie turned away and ran out of the lunchroom. *Dear God!* she prayed. *Please answer me!*

The minute school ended, Jamie raced for her locker. She'd already turned down offers from Harry and Maya to drive her home. She wanted to be alone. She needed to pull herself together.

Jamie shoved history and English books into her locker and loaded her backpack with algebra and science. She turned to go, the clunk of her locker closing echoing behind her.

Outside, the cool breeze made the tiny hairs on her arm stand up. Looping her thumbs through the straps of her backpack, she looked up to glimpse gray clouds hurrying across a sky she might have painted purple with shades of umber.

How many days had she gone without painting or sculpting? She'd spent her art savings on makeup. Why? Because she wanted to be normal, to fit in.

Jamie jaywalked to Cedar Street. *I'd give anything to walk into my house and find Mom laughing from relief, bursting with the good news that Jessica's fine again.*

Isn't that what I'm supposed to expect, God? Jamie wondered, her thoughts and prayers intertwining so she couldn't say where one left off and the other began. *I asked for Jess to be well. Shouldn't I expect You to do it?*

Please Reply!

She stopped in front of her house. Mom's car was parked crooked in the driveway. Jamie took the porch steps slowly. She turned the knob and pushed open the front door, the strip of jingle bells letting out short rings, like gasps.

"Jess? Mom?"

Her mother sat hunched over the kitchen table, her oversized purse tipped over on the floor, pens and Kleenex rolled out over the gray linoleum.

Mom still hadn't turned around. Her shoulders shook as she slurped in air with irregular gulps, like a drowning woman.

Jamie couldn't see her mother's face, couldn't see tears. But she saw enough. She saw enough to know without a single doubt that nothing in her life, nothing in this house, nothing in the world would ever be the same.

chapter.9

Jamie?" Mom wiped her eyes with what was left of her napkin. "I didn't hear you come in." She put on a fake smile that made Jamie want to cry.

"Tell me," Jamie said quietly.

"Oh honey, don't look like that," Mom said. "We don't know anything yet. I guess I fell apart once Jessica fell asleep in her room."

Jamie sat across the table from Mom. The blinds were shut, and it felt like night. "What did the doctor say?"

"Dr. Wheeler couldn't find anything wrong with Jess," Mom said.

"So it's just an infection?" Jamie asked, hoping, praying.

Mom shook her head. "No. Her ears look normal."

Jamie felt hope spark at the word *normal.* "Then she's OK? Her hearing's normal?"

"I didn't say that," Mom corrected. "There's nothing wrong structurally with Jessica's ears." She reached across the table for Jamie's hand.

"But you said—" Jamie pulled her hand away.

"Jessica has lost quite a bit of her hearing," Mom explained. "The doctor thinks the problem is neurological."

"I don't know what that means!" Jamie cried.

Mom took a breath, then seemed to swallow it. "I don't understand it either, honey. Dr. Wheeler said it's another way people can lose their hearing—something to do with brain messages and nerve endings. She set up an appointment with a neurologist this Friday. Until then we just have to pray. It won't do a bit of good to worry."

"And what good will it do to pray?" Jamie blurted out. Her chest burned. "I prayed this would all be over. I prayed Jessica's hearing would be normal. And it's not!"

Mom walked around the table and put her arms around Jamie. "I know how you feel. But honey, God loves Jess even more than we do. He'll see us through this. Let Him."

They weren't just words, not with Mom. Jamie remembered the months of sadness after her dad left. It had felt like the world had crumbled and washed away, leaving nothing to stand on. But they'd survived. And Mom had always given credit to God.

The front door slammed, and Jordan blew in with a gust of wind. A scattering of brown leaves sneaked in behind her. "It's going to storm," Jordan said, throwing her backpack onto the couch. "So what did the doctor say?"

Jamie got up and headed for her room, leaving Mom to handle Jordan. She couldn't sit through another explanation. Once in her room, Jamie automatically turned on her computer. How could she wait until Friday for an answer?

It took her two tries and Spellcheck to spell *neurology* before she could run a search on it. She qualified it with *hearing* and found a dozen medical sites, most of them dealing with kidneys. But she couldn't understand any of the terms. And none of it seemed to apply to Jessica.

Still, Jamie typed into e-mail reply boxes at half a dozen sites: "Could you tell me what kind of hearing loss is neurological?" Then she hit *Please reply* and waited. She waited and waited, but nobody replied.

Jamie felt like crying. She needed answers. Loneliness smothered her. *Why didn't I ask Bren and the others to meet me online?*

She typed "todaysgirls.com" into the location bar and waited for the familiar purple-and-silver logo. At least she didn't feel as alone here. Amber's Thought for the Day popped up, another new one:

. . . If two of you on earth agree about something, then you can pray for it. And the thing you ask for will be done for you by my Father in heaven. This is true because if two or three people come together in my name, I am there with them.—Matthew 18:19-20

Amber had written simply: *We're here for you, Jamie!*

Please Reply!

"That's it!" Jamie exclaimed. *I need help praying! Two or three? I'll get more than that!* She was so excited, her fingers slipped on the keys, and she had to start over logging into the chat room. She just hoped somebody would be there.

Jamie stared at the dialog box, tears sliding down her face, one tear landing on her keyboard. She wiped away the tears with her sleeve as she grinned at her screen. They were all right there waiting for her.

chicChick: we r here 4 U, rembrandt!
faithful1: praying 4 U and Jess, rembrandt!
nycbutterfly: tune in, GF!!
TX2step: me 2 standing by . . .
jellybean: we love U and Jess, rembrandt! JLY!!!!

Jamie said a quick prayer, thanking God for giving her friends like these.

rembrandt: can't Blieve u guys r here!
chicChick: where else would we B???
faithful1: how's Jessica?
TX2step: What did Dr. say?
jellybean: is she ok?

Jamie filled them in on what little news she actually had, responding to their questions more often with "i don't no" than with answers.

rembrandt: faithful1, do U Blieve that verse u have up today about 2 or more agreeing and praying?

faithful1: i believe all the verses in the bible, even tho there R a lot i don't understand. Y?

rembrandt: cuz i need all of u guys 2 pray for Jess with me, that Jess's hearing would go back 2 normal. deal?

jellybean: GR8! Count me in!

chicChick: WOW!! didn't no u could do this! i'm up 4 it! kewl!

TX2step: FWIW i'll give it a shot!

nycbutterfly: i guess. anything 4 Jessica!

faithful1: u bet! God sez we can ask anything. don't 4get that part where he promises 2b with us, rembrandt.

rembrandt: GR8! TTYL! thanx!

Jamie got through the week better than she'd expected. For one thing, she'd never come close to praying this much. Amber probably prayed like this all the time, Jamie suspected. But not the others. Even Maya, who got antsy when anybody mentioned Jesus, met Jamie in the halls with a wink and a point to heaven—Maya's way of saying she was praying.

Tuesday evening Jamie went with Bren to Special Olympics practice only because Jessica insisted. But she surprised herself by enjoying the time. Bren gave another hilarious backstroke lesson, followed by a breaststroke demonstration that had Alan "ROFL."

Jamie spent more time with Leslie and Sandy as the week wore on. Toward the end of one session, Sandy ran up to Jamie so excited she could hardly get the words out. "Did it!" Sandy shouted, out of breath. "Breaststroke! Good!"

"You did the breaststroke well?" Jamie asked, amazed at how happy Sandy looked over such a minor victory.

Sandy laughed. "Not me! Leslie!"

Jamie stared in wonderment. Sandy was this worked up—over somebody else's success? Jamie knew that Sandy couldn't seem to learn the breaststroke. Yet she was bursting with joy because her friend *could?*

Sandy started to walk away, but Jamie called after her, "Sandy, do you pray?"

Sandy's smile grew. She chewed on a wet strand of her auburn hair. "Sometimes at my school, if Leslie and Tina aren't there, nobody talks to me."

Jamie felt like crying, her emotions hovering on the edge of a cliff, waiting for the wind to change. Were these kids teased or worse—the way kids treated Ed?

"But I can always talk to Jesus!" Sandy continued. "Sometimes Michael shouts mean things to my face. But Jesus is deep inside my head, whispering nice things about me."

At school, kids picked up their yearbooks, reminding Jamie about her own problems. Already pictures were being taken for next year, and Jamie made sure she didn't have to shoot the swim team on Saturday. *This time I'm going to be in that picture instead of behind it!*

she determined. Jamie wanted to pave the way for her sisters, to set them on the road to being normal high school students. She owed them that.

Swim team practices never ran smoothly. Harry had lost his whistle, although Jamie was certain she could have located the relic if she'd still been his assistant. Jamie could hardly stand to walk by Coach's office, where papers were piled up and wastebaskets over-flowed. He kept forgetting to bring them schedules, so they couldn't plan for meets.

It wasn't until Thursday after school at the Y that Jamie realized she and Bren had a scheduling conflict. Mrs. Pearson said some-thing about the district meet on Saturday—*this* Saturday.

Bren waved her hand as if they were in class. Then, as she did in school, she blurted out her question anyway. "Jamie and I have an exhibition swim on Saturday and team pictures!"

"Bren, no!" said Mrs. Pearson. "I was counting on you girls to help."

"Sorry," Jamie muttered. And she really was sorry. She'd miss seeing Leslie and Sandy especially and even Ed.

"I'll be here," Alan chimed in. He turned his dreamy eyes on Bren. Jamie could almost see the meltdown.

"Bren," Alan said, "can't you miss swimming just this once?"

Bren smiled over at Alan. "You know, I miss so many practices, I'll bet Coach wouldn't even notice I was gone."

"Bren!" Jamie elbowed her.

"Great!" exclaimed Mrs. Pearson. "How 'bout you, Jamie?"

"'Fraid not," Jamie said. "Sorry." Special Olympics could get along without her.

Bren Mickler will end up in half of the yearbook pictures no matter what, Jamie reasoned. *Bren can afford to skip the swim team shoot. I can't. This is my one chance.*

Friday morning Jamie and Jordan exchanged knowing looks over barely touched bowls of Chocolate Bunny Krisps. Mom was definitely trying too hard to pretend this was an ordinary day, in spite of Jessica's appointment with the neurologist.

"I told you to sleep in today, Jessica," Mom said, pouring herself a glass of juice, even though she already had one on the table.

"Wish someone told *me* that," Jordan said, winking at Jessica.

Jamie felt a surge of love for Jordan. Funny. She and Jordan hadn't had much to say to each other since the onslaught of braces. And now here Jamie sat, nearly stirred to tears because Jordan was trying to make things better for Jess.

"Achoo!" Mom sneezed.

"Bless you," Jordan said.

Mom sneezed twice more.

"You sound bad, Mom," Jamie said.

Mom blew her nose. "Can't seem to get rid of this cold."

"Why can't we just see Dr. Wheeler again, Mom?" Jessica asked. "She's so funny." Jessica turned to Jamie. "She shined this light in my ear and pretended she could see straight through to Mom on the other side."

Harry honked outside, and Jamie got up to leave. She kissed Jessica and Mom good-bye, something she rarely did anymore.

Jordan surprised her by following along outside. "Jessica will be OK, won't she?" Jordan asked, her breath coming out in frost clouds.

Jamie fake-punched her sister's shoulder. "Jess will be fine, Jordan." She turned to go, then wheeled around before Jordan stepped back inside. "Want to walk home together after school?"

Jordan nodded. "Yeah. I'll wait."

Jamie made it through school by sheer grit, talking to God while pretending to take class notes. At lunch, her TodaysGirls buddies were quiet for a change, as if not bringing up Jessica could keep Jamie—or any of them—from worrying.

Jordan was waiting on the cracked sidewalk in front of the middle school when Jamie got there. It felt more like winter than autumn, but neither of them had thought to bring gloves or a warmer jacket.

They walked to the clomping of Jordan's clogs. About a hundred yards from home, Jordan stopped. "What's Harrison Short doing at our house?"

"Harry?" Jamie saw Harry's tan Caravan wheel into the driveway.

"Something's wrong," she muttered, taking off in a dead run.

Harry, out of his car and heading toward the porch, turned. He waved his arms, like an airline worker guiding a plane to its runway.

Jamie didn't stop running until she was in Harry's face. "What is it? What's happened to Jessica?"

Piece by piece her mind took in the clues: Mom's car gone, no lights from the house, Harry still in his school sweats.

"Calm down, Jamie," Coach said, his hands clamping her shoulders. "Jessica's all right."

Jordan ran up, panting, her clogs dangling from one hand. "Where's Jess?"

Harry's eyes looked watery. His thin red hair blew in peaks. He put one hand on Jordan's head. "Your mother called me at school and asked me to meet you two here. She was afraid you'd go nuts when you came home to an empty house."

Jamie struggled to get control of the words that circled in her brain. "Harry," she said, staring through his glasses into his blue eyes. "Where is Jessica?"

Harry glanced from Jamie to Jordan and back again before answering. Then in no more than a whisper, he said, "Jessica is in the hospital."

chapter.10

Jamie stared at Harry, unable to speak.

"Hospital?" Jordan repeated.

"Easy, you two. I can see why your mother sent me to ward you off. Jessica's fine!" Harry's smile looked real, although Jamie knew him well enough to see through to the worry lines at the corners of his mouth.

"Why is she in the hospital, Harry?" Jamie demanded.

"Tests, Jamie. The neurologist wants to give her a couple more tests. And he needs to monitor her overnight. That's all!"

"I want to see her," Jamie said.

"Me too!" Jordan said.

"Then get in." Harry pointed to his car.

Harry drove the speed limit across town. The car had a wet-towel smell. At the first light, Harry checked the rearview. "You girls mind if I pray while I drive?"

Jamie realized that a part of her had been praying nonstop since she'd spotted Harry in her driveway. "Harry," she said, gazing out the window when the light turned green. Other cars, other families, were heading for their normal, safe homes. "I've *been* praying. And it hasn't done any good."

Harry flipped on his turn signal. "It has, Jamie. You have to believe that. We may not always get the answers we want—not in this life anyway—but God hears us."

Without changing his tone, Harry started talking to God. "Father, we admit we're scared for Jessica. Help *her* not to be afraid. Let her know You're with her. You know our desire is to have Jessica hear normally again, to be well, so that's what we pray. And we trust You to answer according to Your perfect will. Amen."

Jamie didn't like the last part of Harry's prayer. She didn't care what God's will was. She wanted her sister to be normal. If anyone deserved a good life, free from illness and handicaps, it was Jessica.

Edgewood Medical Center, a four-story, red-brick rectangle, looked like a factory. Harry parked in the visitors' lot, and they ran in. A blast of hot air hit them as they pushed through the glass revolving door.

Jamie poked the *up* elevator button a dozen times. "I'm taking the stairs," she muttered, leaving Harry and Jordan to wait for the elevator doors to open. She tore up the steps, two at a time, and burst onto the third floor.

Hurrying down the stark, tan hallway, Jamie expected to smell Lysol or antiseptic or chlorine. Instead, she smelled nothing. It was as if the air had been vacuumed, leaving nothing that could make a person sick.

The door to Jessica's room was cracked open. Jamie shouldered it and tiptoed in. The white room was split by a blue curtain that curved around the nearest bed. A group of nurses blocked Jamie's view. She pushed her way through.

"Jamie!" Jessica squealed and held out her arms.

Jamie ran to her sister and hugged her. She heard a cough and turned to see her mother standing at the foot of the bed, a Kleenex over her mouth. "Where's Jordan?"

"They're coming," Jamie said.

"Is this your sister?" asked the tall nurse.

"One of them," Jessica said. "Jamie, these are nurses."

"You're kidding," Jamie said, nodding at them, feeling as if maybe the world wouldn't end after all, now that she could see Jessica for herself.

"Look what they gave me!" Jessica held up two stuffed bears dressed as bride and groom. "Nurses are really nice, except when they stick needles into me."

Jamie touched the cotton hospital nightgown. "Nice outfit, Jess," she teased.

"I can't keep it," Jess said, "which is OK with me because it doesn't close in the back. I get to keep these though!" She stuck her foot, covered in a fuzzy blue sock, in Jamie's face. "See?"

"Whoop-dee-doo!" came a grumpy voice from the other side of the curtain. "What have you got in there, an army? And I can't get a single nurse to move my pillow?"

"Coming, Ms. Teaberry," said a dark-haired nurse, ducking through the curtain.

"I'm sharing my room with Ms. T," Jessica explained.

"I can see that," Jamie said. She felt proud to be related to Jessica, who'd already managed to charm the socks off everybody. *Thank you that Jessica's not afraid,* she prayed.

"Mom! Jess!" Jordan raced in and flung herself at Jessica. Harry followed her in, then moved down next to Mom and tweaked Jessica's toes.

"Thanks, Har—*Achoo!*—Thank you for—*Achoo!*" Mom's sneezes morphed into coughs.

One of the nurses joined Harry and Mom. "Mrs. Chandler," she said, "I know you want to stay with your daughter, but you're not doing her any good with this cold."

"I can't leave Jessica!" Mom sounded pitiful, her voice a scratchy falsetto.

The nurse smiled. "Dr. Casey will look in later, but all Jessica will do tonight is sleep. You don't want to give her your cold."

"Or me!" yelled Ms. Teaberry.

"*I'll* stay with Jess!" Jamie volunteered. She couldn't imagine being anywhere else.

"Can she, Mom?" Jessica asked.

"I'll sleep in this chair," Jamie offered. "Please! I wouldn't sleep at home anyway."

"I don't know, Jamie," Mom started. But she couldn't finish, as sneezes took over. "All right," she said finally.

Jamie and Jess gave each other high-fives.

"What about me?" Jordan whined. "I want to stay, too!"

"You and I will drive back here first thing in the morning," Mom promised.

"Good idea," said the nurse, checking a plastic bracelet around Jessica's wrist. "Jessica needs sleep. She has a big day tomorrow."

Jamie wanted to know exactly what was going into Jessica's "big day." But for now, she'd settle for staying here with Jess.

Harry, Mom, and Jordan made their long good-byes until Ms. Teaberry growled "Good-bye already!" from the other side of the curtain.

Jamie still hadn't seen the woman. She imagined someone fierce, like the Jack-and-the-Beanstalk giant pictured on a book she'd given Jess years ago.

But when she finally got enough nerve to peek behind the curtain, what she saw resembled the beanstalk more than the giant. Ms. Teaberry looked pole-thin under her sheet. She lay on her side, her back to Jamie, a blue plastic mask over her mouth. A ridged tube ran from the mask to a tank. Metal tree poles held plastic bags that dripped liquid through long tubes into both of her arms.

Jamie ducked back behind Jessica's curtain. The whole room

smelled like ice, an unnatural non-smell, a flatness, as if no echo could carry in here.

"Need anything, Jess?" Jamie asked.

"Did you say something?" Jessica asked back.

Jamie crossed over to Jessica and sat on the bed. "You rock, Jess!" she almost yelled. "You know that? What did you do here all day?"

Jessica told Jamie stories of doctors and x-rays, of going from the clinic to the hospital, registering, and finding the room. Jamie marveled at the way Jess talked about everything as a big adventure.

"You're not scared at all, Jess, are you?"

"Not much," Jess said, lifting a white control box and pushing the button to adjust her bed. "Look, Jamie!" Jessica raised the back and foot of the bed, turning it into a recliner.

"Cool," Jamie said, silently thanking God for a bed that made Jess so happy.

"I don't like the needles though." Jessica stretched out both arms to show Jamie the Winnie-the-Pooh Band-Aids covering the needle marks.

Jamie's stomach twinged in sympathetic pain. She had to look away. "Want to watch TV, Jess?" she asked, spying a small television mounted on the opposite wall.

Ms. Teaberry groaned.

"Cool!" Jessica cried, ready for one more adventure. "Would you open the curtain? I want to see how Ms. T is doing."

"Maybe Ms. T needs to sleep," Jamie suggested.

"Go see," Jessica said. She found her TV remote, which also held the speaker for sound. Jessica held it to her ear. "This is as loud as it goes," she said. Jamie could hear the sound well enough from where she sat. She figured the hospital set the volume so patients didn't disturb each other.

Jamie peered behind the curtain. Seeing Ms. T wide awake, she gently pulled back the dividing curtain.

Ms. T frowned over at them. But before the woman could say anything, Jessica shouted, "Ms. T! You're up! Did you meet my sister Jamie? I'm sorry you can't hear the TV over there. Oh—you've got one of your own."

Jessica kept up a stream of chatter. Ms. T didn't say anything, but she didn't tell Jess to shut up either.

After a while, a different nurse brought Jessica dinner—hamburger and fries with a tiny salad and cake. Jamie thought the food looked as plastic as the plates, but Jess ate all her fries and half the burger.

Jessica and the nurse tried to convince Jamie to go to the cafeteria, but she didn't want to leave Jess. So she ate Jessica's spice cake, first scraping off thick white frosting.

Jamie was just moving Jessica's tray away from the bed when a tall, blond man breezed into the room. Instead of a white doctor's coat, he wore an oxford cloth shirt and Dockers. The only clues that he might be a doctor were the stethoscope around his neck and the clipboard tucked under one arm. He didn't even look old enough to be out of college.

"Dr. Casey!" Jessica cried. "Look! We found a TV and a bed button." Jessica turned off the TV and lowered the bed a little.

The man strode to the bed, flashing a movie-star grin, white teeth gleaming from his tanned face. Jamie had the urge to paint him, to see if she could capture the classic chin and strong mouth, his thick hair and deep blue eyes.

"How are we getting along, Jessica?"

"Fine," she answered. "This is my big sister, Jamie. She's staying the whole night!"

He turned his smile on Jamie, sending a shiver through her. *If I were Bren*, Jamie thought, staring stupidly at his outstretched hand, *I'd say something clever*.

Dr. Casey, still smiling, took his hand back. "We better see about getting you a cot in here," he said.

"So, are you sick of me yet?" he asked, turning to Jessica.

She shook her head.

"Good. Sit up straight for me."

Jessica sat on the edge of the bed, her legs swinging. "I like all the doctors," Jessica said. "But your tests are the most fun."

Dr. Casey shined a small flashlight into Jessica's eyes. He had her touch her nose with each index finger, put her fingertips on top of her head, hop off the bed and walk in a straight line, turn, and walk back on tiptoes. He tested reflexes with a small rubber mallet. When he finished, Jessica climbed back in bed and turned on the TV.

Jamie watched the doctor scribble on her sister's chart until she couldn't stand it any longer. Firing up a quick prayer for courage, she walked up to him. "Dr. Casey, what's wrong with my sister?"

He turned a sympathetic smile on her, totally different from the teasing smile he used on Jessica. "I don't have all the answers," he said. "Not yet. That's why we want her here overnight. We'll monitor her rates tonight and do an MRI in the morning, then take it from there."

"An MRI?" Jamie had heard of it. In one TV hospital show, a man got put into a metal tunnel thing. "Why? Why would Jess need that?" She felt her throat tighten, and she gulped.

"Just a precaution," he answered. "Hey, don't look so worried. We're covering all our bases. She's in good hands."

Jamie couldn't help herself. The tears poured down. Her shoulders shook. She turned her back on Jessica.

"Jessica's fine," Dr. Casey said, his voice smooth and confident. He set down the clipboard and put his hands on Jamie's shoulders. Leaning down and fixing his eyes on hers, Dr. Casey whispered, "Trust me, Jamie."

Jamie heard a swish, a bang, and a loud *crash!* She wheeled around, the doctor's hands still on her shoulders.

Bren Mickler stood inside the hospital room, her mouth wide open, her gaze fixed on Jamie and the unbelievably handsome doctor. At her feet lay broken glass and a pile of fallen flowers, but she didn't give them a glance. It was one of the few times Jamie had seen her friend speechless.

"Bren!" Jamie exclaimed.

"I-they-we-flowers," Bren stammered.

Dr. Casey moved to the door, sidestepping the broken vase. He stopped behind Bren and called loudly to Jessica's bed. "Jess! I'll see you tomorrow."

Jessica waved. "Bye! Hey! Hi, Bren!"

"And Jamie," he said in a dreamy, romantic voice Jamie knew was for Bren's sake. "I can't *tell* you how much our time together has meant to me."

Bren gasped.

Dr. Casey winked at Jamie. "Until tomorrow . . ."

chapter.11

Who was that?" Bren cried. "Jamie, you've been holding out on me? He is a major hottie! When did you meet him? It's totally awesome he came here for you at the hospital!"

Jamie knelt down and picked up the daisies, roses, and carnations. "Oh, him? You mean I haven't told you about Casey?"

"Jamie Chandler, tell all!" Bren demanded.

Maya strutted into the room, with Alex and Morgan on her heels. "Who was that fine-looking doctor we saw coming out of here?" She and the others flocked to Jessica's bed.

"Doctor?" Bren muttered. "He's a doctor?"

Jamie laughed. "Yes, Bren. He's a doctor."

"Then he's not—? *You're* not—?"

"We're not," Jamie admitted, picking up the last flower just as a man in a gray uniform came in with a mop.

"Then he's eligible?" Bren asked, rallying.

"Cool," Alex said.

Morgan didn't second Alex's opinion, not with words anyway. But she stood in the doorway, transfixed, staring after the good doctor.

Everybody had presents for Jessica. Morgan and Maya gave her a small cross their mom had made out of silver. Alex brought a sack of black licorice, which Jamie intercepted, since Jessica wasn't supposed to eat until after her morning tests.

"Amber sends her love," Maya said, fastening the cross around Jessica's neck. "She's got this Saturday morning class in Lynchburg, where they teach you how to better your SAT scores. She tried to wiggle out of it, but her dad wouldn't let her. They're staying in Lynchburg tonight and racing back for our swim exhibition."

"What a shame!" Ms. T shouted. "All we need is one more of you."

"Sorry, Ms. T," Jamie called.

"Like Amber needs help on her SATs," Alex said.

"Her dad says she has to make the top 2 percent to get into Harvard Law," Maya explained. "Talk about pressure. But she'll be online for our chat."

"Oops," Morgan said, handing her laptop to Jamie. "Almost forgot. This is for you. We can't chat without you!"

Jamie thanked Morgan. She thanked all of them and wished they didn't have to leave.

"Sorry about the flowers," Bren said.

"They still smell great!" Jessica said, sniffing a rose. "I smelled them before you came in."

"No way!" Bren cried. "I have such horrible smell!"

"Try bathing, Bren," Alex joked.

"Alex!" Bren scolded.

The nurse rolled in a folded bed. "Sorry, girls. Visiting hours ended quite a while ago. Jessica needs sleep. And I need to hook up her monitor."

The mention of the monitor had the effect of a pop-quiz announcement. As the girls left, blowing Jessica kisses, they looked as worried as Jamie felt.

"Don't forget chat tonight," Bren said, coming back to give Jamie another hug. "Jess will be fine."

Jessica fell asleep minutes after being connected to a heart and respiration monitor. Ms. T was already snoring. Mom called three times, with Jamie answering on the first ring and assuring her mother everything was great.

After the last call, Jamie connected Morgan's laptop to the phone jack and logged on to TodaysGirls.com. Amber's Thought for the Day was waiting for her:

Romans 5:3
And we also have joy with our troubles because we know that these troubles produce patience.

Please Reply!

Hang in there, Jamie! Sorry I couldn't be there!—Amber

Jamie wasn't as close to Amber as she was to Bren, or even to Maya and Morgan, since she worked with them at the Gnosh. But she'd have given a lot to have Amber there in person right now so she could ask her what the verse really meant. Jamie still wanted God's answer **now**. She'd never felt less patient.

This time Jamie was the first to sign into the chat room:

rembrandt: i'm here!

A minute later Bren arrived.

chicChick: rembrandt! U K?
rembrandt: how bout u??? ur early!!!!!!!!!!!!!!!
chicChick: FYI i hurried so my best friend wouldn't B alone

Eventually everybody showed up, even Amber arrived from Lynchburg. It was great to chat about nothing, and Jamie didn't want to ruin it with anything heavy. Bren had a hundred questions Jamie couldn't answer about Dr. Casey. Alex said she thought he'd made up the name to sound like some TV doctor her grandmother told her about. Amber said she thought they were making up the whole story starring a high-caliber doctor, just to tease her.

When Jamie signed off and unfolded her bed, she was too hyper to sleep. She lay in the semidarkness, watching lights flicker on Jessica's monitor, squiggly lines measuring her life, her breath, turning everything into numbers. Muffled voices drifted in from the nurses' station.

Lord, she prayed, *I don't want Jess to have to go through what Ed does.*

"Jamie?"

Surprised, Jamie rolled over to face her sister. "Thought you were asleep, Jess."

The monitor emitted a steady *click, click.*

"I was, but I'm not," Jess said, her words floating through the dark. Jamie imagined a stretched canvas, burnt umber brushed to cover the entire background, and pale yellow dots dabbed on for Jessica's soft words. "Whatcha doing?"

"I was praying, Jess," she answered, hoping she was loud enough for Jessica to hear, but not loud enough to wake Ms. T.

Jessica was silent for a minute. Then she said, "Don't you think it's awfully nice of God to be here listening whenever we feel like talking?"

"Um hmm," Jamie said, thinking over the past few days. She never would have believed it was possible for her to pray so much or so often. And she'd known that God was right there with her and with Jess.

. . . I am there in their midst.

Jessica yawned. "Night, Jamie," she said, her words fading into a squeaky yawn. "Love you."

"Love you, too, Jess."

So OK, God, Jamie prayed as she let herself give in to sleep. *I admit You've answered some of my prayers. Thanks for making Jess so brave. And nice job getting me to talk to You this much.*

When Jamie opened her eyes again, Mom and Jordan were in the room talking to a nurse. For a second, Jamie forgot where she was. Then it hit her.

"You're awake," Mom said. She looked beat, with gray circles under her eyes.

Dr. Casey stepped into the room. Jamie fought back her grin when Jordan's jaw dropped, unwittingly revealing the hated braces.

"Morning, Chandler women!" He checked the clipboard that hung by a metal rope from the foot of Jessica's bed. Flipping pages, he hummed. "Everything looks good."

"Wake up!" he shouted, wiggling Jessica's foot through the blanket.

Jessica sat straight up in bed and squinted around. "Morning," she said, a smile for each of them. Nobody woke up sweet like Jess did.

"Ready to get your head examined?" Dr. Casey asked. "Just kidding. Remember what I told you we'd do this morning?"

"MRI, and a sensory . . . something after that," Jessica answered. "And an audience-ologist."

"Audiologist. I wish all of my patients were as smart as you," Dr. Casey said.

A nurse came in with a wheelchair, and Jessica and Dr. Casey left, while the nurse showed Jamie, Jordan, and Mrs. Chandler where to wait.

An hour later, Dr. Casey joined them in the waiting room. "Jessica's fine. She said she loved the tunnel, the MRI. I just have a couple of questions on background to ask you." He pulled a chair around and flipped through his charts. "So, any family history of kidney disease or diabetes?"

"Of what?" Mom's face turned pale. "Does Jess have—?"

"Please, Mrs. Chandler," said the doctor, leaning forward. "I promise you'll know the minute we think we've got Jessica diagnosed. These questions help to eliminate all the possibilities."

"You're right," Mom said. "I understand. I'm sorry."

"Nothing to be sorry about." He waited.

"No diabetes that I know of," Mom answered. "There's nothing wrong with my kidneys or anyone in my family as far as I know."

"How about your husband and his family?"

Jamie's breath grew heavy. She couldn't swallow.

Mom stared at her hands, folded in her lap. "He—we're divorced. I haven't seen Jessica's father for several years. To be honest, I just don't know."

Jamie felt rage as real as concrete, heavy and unbreakable. Her anger grew hotter as Mom tried to answer the rest of the doctor's questions. As soon as he was gone, Jamie blurted out, "I'll bet that's it!"

Jordan frowned at her. "What?"

"I'll bet *he* gave whatever it is to Jessica. I'll bet he had something wrong with him, and now he's passed it on to Jess!"

"You blame Dad for everything!" Jordan snapped.

"Girls, don't!" Mom pleaded.

Jamie started to protest, to tell Mom to stop defending their father, who didn't even have a clue what they were going through because he didn't care. But one look at her mother's anguished face, and Jamie bit her tongue.

"Jessica's problem—whatever it turns out to be—isn't *anybody's fault,*" Mom said wearily. "Get that straight right now. No matter what. Got it?"

Jamie didn't answer, but she gave Mom a look that said she wasn't backing down. It had to be Dad's fault. Jessica had never done anything wrong in her whole life.

"Jamie," Mom said, "you know better. People don't get sick because somebody's done something wrong."

"You don't know that it's not his fault, Mom," she said, no longer able to keep from arguing. "It's sure not Jessica's fault!"

"Of course it's not Jessica's fault!" Mom said. "Listen." Mom opened her purse and searched inside. "Remember that blind man in John? I think it's John 9. Rats! I don't have my Bible with me." She closed her purse. "But you remember that story, don't you?"

"*I* do," Jordan said, as if Jamie had just said she didn't. "The disciples asked Jesus why the man was blind."

Jamie did remember it.

"Right!" Mom said. "They asked Jesus whose fault it was—the

man's or his parents'. And Jesus told them something like, 'It's not this man's fault *or* his parents'. He was born blind so that God's power could be shown in him.'"

The words hung in the air around them as patients shuffled past on their way to radiology, as others were wheeled on gurneys or pushed in wheelchairs. Jamie couldn't get rid of the words: *He was born blind so that God's power could be shown in him.* It was like the sermon verse from Corinthians, the one she hadn't understood: *"When I'm weak, then I am truly strong."*

Jamie didn't think she could ever understand. She was still thinking about the blind man and weaknesses when she heard Jessica's laugh down the hall, and Jess and Dr. Casey joined them. They walked back to Jessica's hospital room together.

"I'm sorry it's been such a long morning," Dr. Casey began, once they'd all found places to sit. "I know this can be as hard on families as it is on patients. But I think we've figured out what's going on with Jessica's hearing."

Jamie held her breath and let her prayers reach out to God in silent pleas.

"We believe your daughter has a neurological disorder called Alport's Syndrome. She's lost 40 percent of her hearing, and the loss is permanent."

chapter.12

"Permanent?" Jamie repeated the word.

She stared at Dr. Casey's mouth as he handed down the diagnosis that felt like a verdict: *The loss is permanent.* She saw his lips move, his tongue bounce against his teeth. She heard words come out: *brain-centered—nerve loss—hereditary.* She heard Jessica's name over and over: *Jessica will need hearing aids. Jessica will adjust with special help. Jessica . . . Jessica . . . Jessica.*

"Wait a minute, please," Mom asked, scooting to the edge of her chair. "How could this happen and we didn't notice it?"

"My guess is you did notice," Dr. Casey said. "Neurological hearing loss can happen overnight. Judging by Jessica's solid articulation, this hasn't been going on long."

He talked on and on, explaining that Alport's Syndrome generally affects kidneys in males. He assured them that only a very few female patients had to worry about this kidney disease. And Jessica's lab work showed her kidneys were fine. He'd want to see her every six months for a while, but he didn't think there was anything to worry about.

Nothing to worry about?

Jamie glanced at Jessica. She was straightening Ms. T's pillows and singing a song she'd learned at school.

"Right now we want to deal with the hearing loss. The audiologist has done her test already. She's arranged for Jessica to leave the hospital with a loaner set of hearing aids. You girls can go hearing aid shopping as soon as everyone's had a chance to get used to the idea."

Terrific, Jamie thought bitterly. *I'm sure all of Jessica's friends will want to go shopping with her.*

"Hey all!" Bren made her entrance in a skin-tight red dress glammed with silver-thread knotwork that matched her silver choker and Celtic knot earrings. Her heels had to be at least three inches high.

"You're gorgeous, Bren!" Jessica exclaimed. "Wow! What a dress!"

"Why, thank you, sweetie!" Bren said, giving Jessica a kiss that left perfect red lips on her cheek. "This old thing?"

She turned her famous smile on Dr. Casey and held out her multi-ringed hand. "I don't believe we've been properly introduced."

The doctor's eyes twinkled as he shook Bren's hand. "Aren't you the flower girl?"

Morgan and Alex burst through the door as if they'd been racing. They were almost as glammed as Bren.

"Just in the neighborhood," Alex said. "Bren? What are *you* doing here?"

Jamie had never seen Alex so dressed up, in hoop earrings big enough to be bracelets. She wore a black knit top cut just above her midriff. And Jamie could have sworn Alex had tamed her hair. Even Morgan looked dressed for the runway, and she hated to dress up.

"What am *I* doing here?" Bren asked. "Don't you guys have a swim exhibition or photo deal or something? I don't have to be at the Y until four."

Behind Morgan, loud clacking sounded, coming closer. "Hey, girl!" Maya strutted into the room, geared up in a backless halter-top and folded scarf over a kerchief hemline skirt. "What are you all doing here?" Behind her, Amber walked in, looking embarrassed but beautiful in an aqua dress.

Jamie's mom joined the group of high-fashion friends, who were blocking the doctor's exit. "How thoughtful of you girls to dress up for Jessica!" she said, putting an arm around Morgan and Alex and leading them out of the way.

It was a relief for Jamie to see Mom smile, and she felt grateful that something this normal could go on in the middle of something so *not.*

Dr. Casey made his getaway, and a few minutes later Mom and Jordan left to sign Jessica out of the hospital. Jamie's friends stayed long enough to hug Jess and Jamie, and left arguing about which one of them looked the most overdressed.

Jamie followed them to the elevators. "See you at the pool. At least I can get in the picture this year."

The elevator came, and the girls stepped on.

Feeling as if a part of her were leaving with her friends, Jamie waved as the doors began to close. "Bye. Bren, tell the Special Olympics kids good luck for me!"

When she got back to the room, Jamie heard Jessica laughing. Ed Spenser was standing by Jess at Ms. T's bed, his back to Jamie.

Ed was shouting, " . . . lost my hearing aid on the playground, and fifty kids landed on it at the foot of the slide before I found it again."

Jamie couldn't remember the last time she'd heard that total, all-out laugh of Jessica's.

"Then," Ed went on, "there was the time I got new ear molds. I think I was your age, Jessica. And I got in class, and my hearing aids were squeaking, but I couldn't hear them. So the teacher wasn't in the room yet. And this little girl who sat behind me thought it was the fire alarm. And she screamed, 'Fire! Fire!' And we all ran out of the room—me too. I thought it was a fire."

Jessica hung on every word. Even Ms. T grinned at Ed.

The audiologist came in to fit Jessica's hearing aids, and Ed told Jessica good-bye. Jamie was still standing in the doorway when he came out.

Ed smiled at Jamie, and she realized that it was the first time he'd looked directly at her. "Jessica's in good hands," he said. "Dr. Casey's cool."

"You know Dr. Casey?" Jamie asked. *Of course he knows him,* she thought a second later. *Ed and Jess both . . .* She didn't want to finish the thought, didn't want Jessica to have anything in common with Ed, not even a doctor.

Ed didn't bother answering. "Jamie," he said, "it's not so bad."

Jamie couldn't explain, even to herself, why Ed's words, his pitying *her,* made tears rush to her eyes with the force of flood waters. She stepped out into the hall so Jessica couldn't see her cry. "I . . . I don't want Jess to be handicapped. I'm sorry, Ed. I just don't. She shouldn't have to go through this. It's not fair!"

Of all the people in the world, why am I telling him this? Ed? Special Ed! She wanted to apologize. But she couldn't. She meant every word of it.

Ed smiled down at her. "That's how I felt. You know what Dr. Casey told me? He said that someday we'd all get perfect bodies. But down here on earth, we're all handicapped—just in different ways. It's not our disabilities that make us who we are. It's what we do with them."

"What does he know?" Jamie snapped. "What would a doctor who looks like that know about being handicapped?"

"All Dr. Casey ever wanted to do was play baseball. Did he tell you that?" Jamie shook her head. "But he had something wrong with his heart. He's OK, but he's not supposed to run fast. His brother plays in the minors in Philadelphia."

Jamie sniffed, trying to stop crying.

Ed went on. "Dr. Casey says he knows that God used his heart problems to make him who he is . . . which is a very good doctor who will take good care of Jessica."

Ed glanced at his watch. "I better go. Mrs. Pearson wants us to get to the Y early."

Jamie watched him amble off down the hall, his gait stiff and irregular. He passed a group of people. Two of them turned to stare after Ed.

Jamie felt a stab in her heart. *No,* she thought. *Not Jessica. Not my Jess.*

As they gathered Jessica's stuff to leave, Jess said good-bye to Ms. Teaberry. She kept pushing the plastic bean part of her hearing aids over her ears. But already she'd stopped talking too loud.

"Go ahead, Ms. T," she said, standing inches from her head. "What's another word for hard water?"

Ms. T made a grumbling noise that rattled her chest into a cough. "If it's not H_2O, I give up."

"Ice!" Jessica laughed so hard her hearing aids squeaked. She leaned down and kissed Ms. T's dry, wrinkled cheek. "We'll come back and visit you. I promise."

Mom drove straight home. "You'd better hurry, Jamie," she said as they pulled up the driveway. "Harry wants you suited up by 3:30. I know! We'll all go. That sound good, girls?" She turned off the engine and looked back at Jordan.

Jordan shrugged, then nodded, back to keeping her closed-lips vow. Jessica was already shouting, "Go, Jamie!"

Jamie grabbed the sacks of dirty clothes and plastic junk from the hospital and headed in. "I probably won't even get to swim," she said. "I'm going mainly to get my picture taken with the team."

"We don't mind, do we, girls?" Mom said as she unlocked the door to the house.

Jessica raced in first. "I wish your thing wasn't the same time as Ed's meet. Don't you hope he gets to State?"

Jamie grabbed her swimming gear and got ready as fast as she could. She wondered how Ed and the others were feeling. Would Sandy remember how to float? Would brave Leslie try the breast-stroke with only one good arm? How would Ed do in the back-stroke when he hadn't had much time to practice? And Tina?

When Jamie came out of her room, swim bag in hand, she looked down the hallway into the kitchen. Jessica was sitting at the table with a plateful of crackers and cheese. She had her hair pulled back in a ponytail under her baseball cap. With her ears completely uncovered, Jessica's hearing aids stuck out like advertisements.

"Jessica," Jamie said, a false cheeriness in her voice, "why don't I fix your hair?"

Jessica shrugged and kept eating.

Jordan came out of the bathroom as Jamie pulled off Jessica's cap and let down her ponytail. Jamie ran her fingers through the fine, black hairs, directing the strands over Jessica's ears, hiding the hearing aids.

"I liked your hair better in a ponytail, Jess," Jordan said, frowning directly at Jamie.

Jamie didn't say anything. *I have to do everything I can,* she told herself. *I have to keep Jessica normal.*

They piled into the car, and Mom drove to school. Mom and the girls climbed the bleachers while Jamie headed for the locker room.

Coach Short called to her as she hurried by. "Jamie! Wait!"

Jamie came back. She was afraid to start talking to Harry, afraid to tell him everything locked in her mind. If she opened it, if she started, could she ever stop?

"So?" he asked. "How did it work out for Jessica?"

Jamie glared at him. "It *didn't* work out, Har—Coach! Jessica won't get her hearing back. She has to wear hearing aids. She has no idea what that's going to mean to her, how kids are going to make fun of her."

"And you do?" Harry said quietly.

"Yeah!" Jamie was already running for the locker room. She didn't want him to see her cry. She had to be strong, strong for Jess.

"Jamie!" Coach called after her.

But she wouldn't stop. She wasn't his assistant. She was part of the *regular* swim team. Jess would be regular, normal, too. *And it's up to me to see that she is!*

chapter.13

"Hey, girl!" Maya shouted when Jamie strode into the locker room. "Suit up!"

The other girls greeted her on their way out, pouring out of the room like a raging river, leaving Jamie alone.

"Coming!" Jamie called after them. She could change in under a minute. As she tugged on her suit, Jamie thought about Leslie from Special Olympics, who took fifteen minutes to suit up. Leslie always insisted on doing it herself. And she never seemed impatient or frustrated.

Jamie's mind flashed back to Amber's verse about troubles making people patient. Leslie was living proof of that.

Zandrea stuck her head into the locker room just as Jamie threw her clothes into her locker. "Jamie! We're lining up!"

"OK!" Jamie hurried to the door, glancing at the mirror on her way past. She was struck by how normal she looked. *How can I look so regular on the outside,* she marveled, *when I feel like a walking explosion?*

Instead of supervising the team photo, Jamie sat in the chair between Zandrea and Morgan as a disembodied voice came over the loudspeakers. "Please welcome Edgewood High School's premier swim team!" As each swimmer's name was announced, spectators offered polite applause.

Jamie pictured Bren at the Y. *Are they getting announced now, too?*

Zandrea leaned over and whispered, "Did you see Amber? I think she looks tired. Bet I can beat her time today."

Jamie knew all the Special Olympics kids would be cheering for each other, wholeheartedly hoping the best for their teammates.

"Jamie Chandler, sophomore!" said the announcer.

Above the applause, Jamie detected Jordan's whistle. She craned her neck until she spotted her family in the middle bleachers. Jessica waved. Her hair fell across her face, and she pushed it back then continued clapping.

Suddenly Jamie wanted to run to them. She wanted nothing more than to climb the bleachers and pull Jessica's hair back into a ponytail. Maybe those hearing aids . . . maybe they were part of something bigger than Jamie, bigger than Jessica. Maybe, like Ed said, how Jessica handled her hearing problem, her *handicap*, would help make her the person God wanted her to be.

Dan, the other freelance photographer for the yearbook, moved in closer and popped the lens cap off his camera.

"Do I have lipstick on my teeth?" Zandrea asked.

Jamie glanced at her. Ed's words came back: *We're all handicapped.* Maybe the need to look perfect, to be popular—maybe that was a kind of handicap. *I ought to know,* she thought. *And Zandrea might have handicaps I can't even imagine.*

"Well, how do I look?" Zandrea asked.

Everybody is handicapped down here on earth. Or maybe nobody really is.

Not being Bren, not being rich, not having a dad around—those aren't my handicaps. It's being ungrateful for how You created me, Father.

And again, her thoughts had transformed into prayer. *Thank You, God! Be strong in my weaknesses. I've got plenty of them for You to work with!* She thought about what she'd just prayed. *Man, am I bragging about weakness?*

"Jamie!" Zandrea cried. "Rewind! Do I—"

Jamie jumped to her feet. "I have to go."

"You *can't* go!" Zandrea protested. "Look! He's trying to take our picture."

"Morgan!" Jamie turned to her. "I'm going to the Y. I have to see the kids swim."

"Now?" Morgan asked. "You're going now?"

"Jamie?" Maya leaned forward and gazed down the row of swimmers.

"Guys," Jamie said, making eye contact with Amber, Alex, and Maya. "I have to go help with Special Olympics! I'm sorry."

"Don't be sorry," Amber said. "Go!"

"Tell them I'm cheering for them, too!" Morgan cried.

"You sure?" Alex asked. "You'll miss pictures."

"I've never been more sure of anything!" Jamie said.

She raced to Harry, wondering how much of the conversation he'd overheard. "Coach," she said, grabbing onto his arm. "I've loved swimming on the team, but I want my old job back. Is that OK?"

"OK? Are you kidding? My wife, my boys, and the whole team thank you! I can't find anything in my office. But are you sure, Jamie?"

"Positive!" Jamie wrapped her towel around her. She wouldn't have time to change clothes. "I have to see the Special Olympics team."

"Go then!" he yelled after her.

Jamie turned and smiled at him. "Bye, **HARRY!**" she shouted, dashing into the locker room to gather her gear.

She stormed the bleachers and grabbed Jessica's and Jordan's hands.

"Jamie!" Mom exclaimed. "What on earth—?"

"Hurry!" Jamie cried. "Mom, we have to get to the Y!"

"What about your team?" Mom asked, scurrying to keep up as they stepped down the bleachers.

"I'm going back to being Harry's assistant," she answered, leaping the rest of the way down and catching Jessica in her arms. Everything felt so right, and Jamie silently thanked God for helping her see it.

Please Reply!

Jessica's hearing aid squawked as she slid into the backseat with Jamie, leaving Jordan to man shotgun. "Sorry," Jessica said, poking the earpiece farther inside her ear.

"Don't be sorry, Jess," Jamie said. She shivered as her bare back leaned against the cool vinyl car seat. She spotted her Indians baseball cap on the back dash. "Here, Jess! Let's get you a ponytail."

Jamie pulled Jessica's hair back, exposing the hearing aids, stuck on the cap, and pulled Jess's hair through the back hole. She leaned back and stared at the plastic tubes that connected the bean part to the ear mold, the amazing contraption that let Jess hear lockers slam and birds sing.

"You know," Jamie said, "those hearing aids are awesome. Mind if I borrow them sometime?"

Jamie barely noticed the cold as her bare feet crossed the tar lot and sped up the sidewalk into the Y. They burst into the pool area just as swimmers were being lined up for the first heat.

"That's Ed!" Jessica cried, pointing toward the starting blocks. "He's swimming first!"

Ed was walking to the blocks, the middle in a pack of five swimmers.

"Let's sit over there behind the team," Mom said. She and Jordan moved to the home bleachers.

Jessica and Jamie stood waving at Ed, trying to get his attention.

"He doesn't see us!" Jessica said.

Jamie moved closer. "Ed!"

A dozen heads turned to stare at her, but she didn't care. "Ed!"

she screamed, wondering what it would take to make him hear. She had to make him hear, to let him know they were cheering for him, to let him know she understood now what he meant.

Jamie moved closer, she and Jessica yelling for Ed with all their lung-power.

"Jamie!" Sandy cried. "You came!"

Then Bren ran up and hugged her. "I thought you were getting your picture taken!"

Jamie returned the hug. "I've been such an idiot, Bren! I couldn't have lived with myself if I hadn't come."

Jamie turned to see Ed step up on the starting block. "Ed!" she screamed, and her heart prayed God would make Ed hear.

Whether Ed heard or saw, Jamie didn't know. But he stopped swinging his arms and frowned their way. When their eyes met, Ed's frown changed into a huge smile.

"He sees us!" Jessica cried. "Good luck, Ed!"

The whole Special Olympics team, including Bren and Jamie, cheered as swimmers were called to their marks. The starting gun fired, and shouts broke out as the swimmers dived in.

Ed surfaced in second place. Jamie couldn't hear herself yell above the steady roar of the crowd. Ed kept his strokes even and steady until the very end, when he edged past his opponent.

"Ed won!" Jessica screamed.

The swimmers helped one another out of the water, congratulating even the last-place swimmer as if he'd won the Olympic gold.

"Ed's a winner!" Bren cried.

"They're all winners, Bren," Jamie said, elated in this new understanding. "I'd be proud to swim on this team, wouldn't you?"

For the rest of the meet, Bren and Jamie helped swimmers to their marks. Each race carried its own drama, its own victories. When Sandy didn't want to get into the water, the judges held off the start until Jamie could slip into the pool and coax her in. Sandy swam the race, finishing a full two minutes behind the other swimmers. But when she reached the end, she got a standing ovation. Parents, spectators, coaches, and even opposing swimmers cheered.

When the meet ended and Jamie and Jessica joined Mom and Jordan in the bleachers, Mom was crying. "Weren't they wonderful!" Mom said between sobs.

Ed walked up, and when Jessica smiled at him, her hearing aids squawked. Ed grinned back, then cupped his hand over his ear to set off his own hearing aid.

Maybe Jessica's hearing loss would never make sense. But a lot of things *did.* Seeing the joy around her, Jamie couldn't help but praise God for *His power made perfect in weakness.* She'd learned so much from them, from Ed, and from Jess.

Jamie gazed back at the swimmers, who were hugging each other, all so happy it was impossible to tell which ones had won and which had lost. *There's more joy per square inch here than anyplace I've ever been,* she thought.

Jamie grinned at Jordan. Even Jordan, who had sworn never to smile again until her braces came off, couldn't resist what was going on here. Her smile was so big her braces sparkled like inexplicable hope.

Epilogue

rembrandt: amazing day!!

chicChick: u can say that again!! congrats to u swimmers! GR8 times!

nycbutterfly: Thanx! everybody ruled except Zandrea. She came in dead last & whined about it

TX2step: 1st place here, thank u very much!

faithful1: we no we no!

jellybean: sorry i missed Ed & all

chicChick: it was the best!

rembrandt: i learned a ton! like about handicaps

nycbutterfly: i hate that word--handicap.

rembrandt: its not so bad really. your handsome Dr Casey sez we all have handicaps. i think he's right.

TX2step: NW! not me! 1st place here!

faithful1: go on, rembrandt

rembrandt: my handicap is i don't feel normal. i can't think of quick, funny things to say. i don't feel like i fit in half the time

chicChick: don't say that!

jellybean: yes u do!!

faithful1: we love U just like U R, rembrandt! if that's not normal, then don't b normal!!!!

TX2step: i can't Blieve this! U don't think UR normal? i thought i was the only 1

jellybean: i no i'm not as kewl as my brainy sister. sometimes that feels like a handicap.

TX2step: hey, ur sister IS your handicap!!!

nycbutterfly: thanx, 2step! jellybean, get real! i'd give anything 2 have ur peaceful, easy-going life! or 2B smart as faithful1 or paint like rembrandt! i no i tend to run over people. some MIGHT call it bossy. but what about faithful1? no handicap there!!!

faithful1: guys! r u kidding? my handicap is trying to live up to what people think. U no, rembrandt's right. we've all got weaknesses. but i think God did a GR8 job on all of us!

rembrandt: RO!

Jamie thought about Amber's verse. *When I'm weak, then I'm strong.* It made more sense now. She'd seen it in Ed. His weakness, his hearing loss, had somehow made Jessica's problem easier. He'd known how to help her when her own sister couldn't. Maybe part of the reason the Special Olympics kids experienced such pure joy had to do with learning through their handicaps.

TX2step: hey! anybody else notice we've all fessed up
    on r problems--all except chicChick???

nycbutterfly: yeah! what about it, chicChick??

chicChick: o all right . . . u may not have noticed, but i'm
    a little clumsy . . .

rembrandt: never noticed . . .

TX2step: LOL

nycbutterfly: ROFL! go on!

chicChick: and i have 2 warts. promise not 2 tell!!!!

jellybean: we won't tell!!

rembrandt: hmmm maybe i can help. i'll phone Dr.
    Casey and ask him what to do about your clumsiness
    & warts.

chicChick: don't u dare!!! i nu i shouldn't have told! now
    u won't want 2B friends with me!

Jamie shot up a quick prayer of thanks for all of her friends.

rembrandt: r u kidding??? i love all of you--warts and
    all!!!

Net Ready, Set, Go!

I hope my words and thoughts please you.
Psalm 19:14

The characters of TodaysGirls.com chat online in the safest—and maybe most fun—of all chat rooms! They've created their own private Web site and room! Many Christian teen sites allow you to create your own private chat rooms, and there are other safe options.

Work with your parents to develop a list of safe, appropriate chat rooms. Earn Internet freedom by showing them you can make the right choices. *Honor your father and your mother (Deuteronomy 5:16).*

Before entering a chat room, you'll select a user name. Although you can use your real name, a nickname is safer. Most people choose one that says something about who they are, like Amber's name, faithful1. Don't be discouraged if the name you select is already taken. You can use a similar one by adding a number at its end.

No one will notice your grammar in a chat room. Don't worry if you spell something wrong or forget to capitalize. Some people even misspell words on purpose. You might see a sentence like How R U?

But sometimes it's important to be accurate. Web site and e-mail addresses must be exact. Pay close attention to whether letters are upper- or lowercase. Remember that Web site addresses don't use some punctuation marks, such as hyphens and apostrophes. (That's why the "Today's" in TodaysGirls.com has no apostrophe!) And instead of spaces between words, underlines are often used to_make_a_space. And sometimes words just run together like onebigword.

Please Reply!

When you're in a chat room, remember real people are typing the words that appear on your screen. Treat them with the same respect you expect from them. Don't say anything you wouldn't want repeated in Sunday school. *Do for other people what you want them to do for you (Luke 6:31).*

Sometimes people say mean, hurtful things—things that make us angry. This can happen in chat rooms, too. In some chat rooms, you can highlight a rude person's name and click a button that says, "ignore," which will make his or her comments disappear from your screen. You always have the option to switch rooms or sign off. If a particular person becomes a continual problem, or if someone says something especially vicious, you should report this problem user to the chat service. *Ask God to bless those who say bad things to you. Pray for those who are cruel (Luke 6:28–29).*

Remember that Internet information is not always factual. Whether you're chatting or surfing Web sites, be skeptical about information and people. Not everything on the Internet is true. You don't have to be afraid of the Internet, but you should always be cautious. Practice caution with others even in Christian chat rooms.

It's OK to chat about your likes and dislikes, but *never* give out personal information. Do not tell anyone your name, phone number, address, or even the name of your school, team, church, or neighborhood. Be cautious. . . . *You will be like sheep among wolves. So be as smart as snakes. But also be like doves and do nothing wrong. Be careful of people (Matthew 10:16–17).*

Cyber Glossary

Bounced mail An e-mail that has been returned to its sender.

Chat A live conversation—typed or spoken through microphones—among individuals in a chat room.

Chat room A "place" on the Internet where individuals meet to "talk" with one another.

Crack To break a security code.

Download To receive information from a more powerful computer.

E-mail Electronic mail sent through the Internet.

E-mail address An Internet address where e-mail is received.

File Any document or image stored on a computer.

Floppy disk A small, thin plastic object that stores information to be accessed by a computer.

Hacker Someone who tries to gain unauthorized access to another computer or network of computers.

Header Text at the beginning of an e-mail that identifies the sender, subject matter, and the time at which it was sent.

Home page A Web site's first page.

Internet A worldwide electronic network that connects computers to each other.

Link Highlighted text or a graphic element that may be clicked with the mouse in order to "surf" to another Web site or page.

Log on/Log in To connect to a computer network.

Modem A device that enables computers to exchange information.

The Net The Internet.

Newbie A person who is learning or participating in something new.

Online To have Internet access. Can also mean to use the Internet.

Surf To move from page to page through links on the Web.

Upload To send information to a more powerful computer.

The Web The World Wide Web or WWW.